OUT OF THE WHIRLPOOL

# The Harper Short Novel Series

———————————

CUTS
*by Malcolm Bradbury*

BLACK SWAN
*by Christopher Hope*

FROZEN MUSIC
*by Francis King*

THE LADIES OF MISSALONGHI
*by Colleen McCullough*

HEARTSTONES
*by Ruth Rendell*

NIGHTS AT THE ALEXANDRA
*by William Trevor*

THE RULES OF LIFE
*by Fay Weldon*

### By the same author

*Novels*

Saturday Night and Sunday Morning
The General
Key to the Door
The Death of William Posters
A Tree on Fire
A Start in Life
Travels in Nihilon
Raw Material
The Flame of Life
The Widower's Son
Her Victory
The Storyteller
The Lost Flying Boat
Down from the Hill
Life Goes On

*Short Stories*

The Loneliness of the Long Distance Runner
The Ragman's Daughter
Guzman, Go Home
Men, Women and Children
The Second Chance

# ALAN SILLITOE

## OUT OF THE WHIRLPOOL

ILLUSTRATIONS BY PETER FARMER

1817

HARPER & ROW, PUBLISHERS, New York

*Cambridge, Philadelphia, San Francisco, Washington*
*London, Mexico City, São Paulo, Singapore, Sydney*

FIRST U.S. EDITION 1988

*Designer: Lydia Link*

---

Library of Congress Cataloging-in-Publication Data

Sillitoe, Alan.
  Out of the whirlpool.

  (Harper short novel series)
  I. Title.
PR6037.I55O98   1988        823'.914        87-45850
ISBN 0-06-015892-1

---

88 89 90 91 92 MPC 10 9 8 7 6 5 4 3 2 1

The man that wandereth out of the way of understanding shall remain in the congregation of the dead.

Proverbs 20:16

# PART ONE

CRANE WITH A BALL AND CHAIN came up over the cobblestones and got into position. The man in the cab worked wheels and levers, and didn't smile like Peter when the solid ball swung against walls and windows.

The dull impact had no effect at first, but the small bricks gave way before the second blow, the ball slewing over the top of the heap it had made. Towards the back of the house, helped by the join where it met the scullery, another strike was needed, and Peter fancied that above the motor noise he heard the driver laugh as he decided on the house's final doom.

Each thump of the ball against solid bricks made his heart shudder, though the effect was not unpleasant. He had always lived in that sort of house, and in a year or two its turn would come. A cloud of orange dust mingled with the summer blue of the sky.

You learned nothing by watching old houses being knocked down, but he enjoyed the spectacle, and felt that what you liked doing taught you more than being in school. Walking after the motorised crane took the ache out of his legs, and when one dwelling went, he wanted two, and then three, to go. He felt so much part of the street that nobody bothered him. A woman and two idle men also watched, as well as a few snotty kids who couldn't appreciate what was happening with the same intensity as himself.

When the crane moved, he moved. A slithering outside wall revealed blue wallpaper, as well as the black fireplace and a chimney column going through the house. A room which seemed big from his bed, when he thought a ghost was on its way up the stairs, covered no more space than a handkerchief, and made his heart beat almost as loud as when the ball struck the whole edifice into dust.

He didn't know whether to go home and get something to eat, or stay and see one more wall go down. The fall and crumble of each house didn't finally satisfy him. He craved to witness a spectacular annihilation more inspiring than what had gone before, a house pulled out by the roots so that not even rubble remained.

His mother had promised him a watch, but only to stop his pestering. He needed one to tell what time it was. The snotty-nosed kids had gone, and so had the woman with folded arms. When a short, tubby bloke in a jersey and cap took over from the man in the crane, Peter knew it was after midday.

A man wearing a trilby hat and a raincoat, even though it was hot and dry, stood by the curb, and when Peter asked what time it was he looked at his wristwatch. 'What do you want to know for?'

His belly rumbled. 'Is it dinnertime?'

The driver sorted his levers, and began where the other left off. He had glasses and a podgy face.

'It's twenty past twelve, if you want to know.'

The great iron ball exposed a room with a gas stove, which on hitting the dust in a cloud of plaster and bricks made them both laugh.

'Are you hungry?'

He was clammed, but said nothing. Maybe he was the truant officer, and would tell his mother. The man stood right next to him. 'I saw worse things in the war. I had to dig bodies out after the air raids. I wasn't much older than you. I was a cadet in the civil defence.'

There were no bodies in the houses being smashed down, and that was a fact. Unable to look and listen at the same time, he hoped the man would go away. His mother was too badly to care, though if she did cry about him not going to school he wouldn't like it, because he hated to see her in tears. 'Why don't you fuck off and leave me alone?'

The crane noise didn't smother the man's laugh. 'Ah! I'd have expected no less from you. That's just what I would have said at your age. If you're hungry, though, you'd better come with me. I'll tek you to a caff and buy you some pastries.'

Peter saw visions of as good a feed as he sometimes thought about on going to sleep at night, wondering what might be for breakfast. When he stayed at his grandma's, she fed him lumpy porridge, though one morning when there was none left she went to the corner shop and bought cornflakes, which were marvellous.

His mother had a bad back that wouldn't get better. The doctor gave her pills but she still groaned all night, so she wouldn't want to hear that he hadn't gone to school.

The crane and ball came his way again. In the next street another machine was doing the same, and two streets away similar clouds of dust shot up, as if the whole district was falling down.

*  *  *

A pebble dash of ice and snow covered the old lime kilns near the canal, bricks scattered like pieces of thrown-away cake. You could see where the oven doors had been. A black and white Jack Russell ran along the bank, chased by a black collie. Maybe they were after each other. If they did it in the street and got stuck, women ran out with buckets of water to part them.

His heels couldn't crumble the ice. Tread without looking, and you slipped. Few people were about, and not much traffic on the road leading to the three streets known as Radford Woodhouse.

He forgot his freezing feet, and his body aching from the cold, and stared at a mountain range of cloud reaching the top of the sky and blocking the road off from whatever was beyond. A pale candyfloss of train smoke hovered behind the chimney pots.

Albert the milkman pushed a bike with a churn on each handlebar. His bulging raincoat covered lots of jerseys, and Peter heard the slop of the milk, unable to understand why it wasn't as frozen as the water on the canal. 'I want a lad to come round with me and push the bike.'

So what? Peter said to himself.

'How old are you?'

'Fourteen.'

Clouds were either there or they weren't. It rained or it didn't. When it snowed they weren't visible. If they were high, the teacher said, they would go away. An Antarctic landscape had drifted from the South Pole, and the sight awed him. Albert straightened his cap. 'I'll give you a quid for a couple of hours' help on Saturday morning.'

His mother would call him daft for turning down a job. How could he save up for a radio if he didn't earn some money? She'd had another operation. 'Now they've sent me home to die.' He hoped not, though everybody did if they were ill long enough. So he didn't want to be out at work if it happened.

'You're a strong lad,' Albert said.

He wouldn't be able to hold the old grid steady, prophesied a flood of milk down the gutter as the handlebars yanked out of his grip. He'd spend the rest of his life paying the damage. Next year he would go to work and get real wages.

'Do you know anybody else as wants a job, then?'

He didn't, so Albert manoeuvred his load along the icy road, his tread dying before he had gone a few yards. The last sound was his breath puffing through a cigarette.

With little effort you could climb in and explore the clouds. But he'd be badly equipped on ice so slippy he wouldn't be able to stand. He might never stumble out of the valleys, get lost in caves, fall from high peaks and not know when he had reached bottom because he would be dead. Without cap or topcoat he'd die in no time, and there'd be no grandmother's house close by with tea on the table and bread steaming at the bars of the fire.

The landscape of cloud had been put there for him, though to get to a point where he could step into it would be hard because the cotton-wool continent drew tantalisingly back. He would flounder in the icy wilderness, always hoping to see blue sky beyond the next rounded peak.

'You'd better get moving, kid,' a gruff voice said, 'or you'll freeze to death.' Jacob Foster was a collier who lived next door but one to his grandma. Peter had a note for her in his pocket, and delivering it was a task which seemed as good as any to begin the day, as he watched Jacob blundering down the lane to keep warm.

He'd read the note while passing Radford station, so short that his mother might as well have told him what to say instead of writing. She was badly, and could no longer manage to get out of bed even to go to the lavatory. She'd had a breast off, and her back was still killing her. So come as soon as you can. I've got nobody else to turn to.

✻   ✻   ✻

The place where they burned bodies was on a hill, and he went through the cemetery in a motor car. He wore a suit and had his hair parted. His grandma held his hand all the way from the house to getting out at the chapel, where they found bunches of flowers and a wreath from the neighbours. I wish she wouldn't keep holding my bloody hand. 'It's not much use buying him a suit because he'll grow out of it too soon.'

'I suppose we'd better, though,' Len said. 'He's hardly got a bit o' rag to his arse.'

Wind flew at the gravestones as if to blow flowers out of the vases. Four men in posh suits pushed the coffin on a trolley into the building that was like a castle on the outside and a church on the inside.

Tall, red-faced and white-haired, Len stood rigidly at the back, as if he was a stranger who had come in out of the wind rather than a man at the funeral of his woman's daughter. He wore a navy blue suit and a chrysanthemum in his buttonhole that his grandma had told him to take out because it wasn't suitable for the occasion. Len used to work in a factory but now washed plates in the canteen. He couldn't read or write, and didn't like anybody who could, so he must have been a real duffer at school, if ever he had gone.

Peter thought about his mother. Do you know what they did? He would tell her. It was like that. It was like this. Oh stop it, she'd say, while I get your tea. You talk the hind leg off a donkey.

He couldn't make himself cry. They'd laugh at school if they found out. Your mam's gone away and won't come back, his grandma said. Until you brought home a wage packet they treated you like an idiot.

He wanted to get a job and go away. His mother was dead because he had seen her dead. She once tried to make him sick when he swallowed a button, shook a packet of salt into a cup of hot water, but it hadn't worked. Nobody knew what happened to the button.

The parson told them to sit down. Why did they do as he said? His grandmother pulled him to the seat and gave him a book. No pictures. 'Behave yourself.'

'Why?'

'You're in the House of God, that's why.'

'So what?'

'Your mother's watching you.'

The parson jawed about Joyce Winifred Granby, saying what a wonderful person she was, though he'd never known her. The coffin was in front of a red curtain. If she could see she could also hear, but she could neither see nor hear because she was dead and they were going to cremate her. He didn't know whether it was better to be eaten by worms or burned to ash so that not even a skeleton was left.

The door opened, which stopped the parson in mid-prayer, as mad as if he'd like to cremate whoever banged it so loud. Peter hoped he would let them go home, but his grandma gripped his hand so that he couldn't yank it away. 'I can't think what he's doing here,' she whispered, pulling him to his feet when they were told to stand.

The man behind was the bloke in the mackintosh and nicky hat he'd met when they were knocking down houses. His hat was off, and he was bald except for a few dark strings across pink skin. His mam called him blind because he'd left her when Peter had been a baby, gone off to London with his fancy woman, who had three kids of her own. He was a rotter. He'd got no heart. He'd given up a good job in a warehouse to swan off with his fancy woman, who was all red hat and no drawers.

She told him till he couldn't be bothered to listen, though he'd kill him as soon as he could. He gave me a kid and left me to struggle on my own. That's the sort of man your dad is—or was. Never a penny for Christmas or birthdays. Not even a letter. They got national assistance and supplementary benefits and anything she could bluff out of the social workers such as boots and overcoats. But he won't prosper, I'm sure of that. Her voice was even louder now that she was dead.

Peter hadn't told her his father had a car, because she was badly and it would make her worse. He meant to wait till she got better, but now it was too late, unless they met in heaven, which they might if there was such a place.

His father had treated him to a hot dinner and ice cream. If he told his mother, she would carry on and shout. When he got home her back was so bad they had to send for a doctor because she had fainted.

The musty smell was from her body, and if it got stronger it would make him sick. Then he knew it was the place that stank and not her. Years of rotting flowers and hot breath had brewed it up.

They read from the book about God and Dust. Words were in front of his eyes, but his lips stayed closed. Tears crinkled the paper, and her hands shook. He couldn't tell whether it was due to his mother being dead or because his father was standing behind.

In the café he scoffed his plate empty in no time. His father only had a cup of tea, and asked about his mother. Somebody had told him she was ill.

'Are you coming home, then?'

'Not after what I did. I'll leave her in peace.'

'What about your fancy woman?'

'You'd better finish that ice cream, and I'll tek yer back where I found yer.'

The streets were a smoking ruin. He wanted to go with his father, anywhere. He wanted to ask him to come home, but his mother would create ructions. A column of lorries took rubble away. They were making an aerodrome, or filling in a canal. His mother would hate him evermore if he went back with his dad. Piles of window frames were set alight, sparks crackling. He could hardly see in the smoke. Men sat joking because it was the end of the day.

They sang a hymn about Jerusalem. It was in Israel. Your mam liked it, his grandma said, but it must have been before he was born, or before she met his father. The half dozen of them read the words, but his father's voice was so loud it drowned everybody else.

Give me my arrows of desire and my chariots of fire. Peter joined in because he wouldn't be noticed. Or maybe he wanted to be heard by his mother. His father's voice rolled on like splintering wood, as if he was the only one with a right to sing, wanting to blot out what he'd done to his mother.

It was as too late as not having told her about meeting his father by the demolition site. And now he was standing behind and bawling his head off at her funeral. The hymn wouldn't go on forever, thank God.

His father didn't even reach the last line. It was as if he had been standing on the edge of a cliff, then went tumbling over, hitting bushes and boulders, and plunging into a swirling river that would take him into hell. The cry shocked everyone, because his grandmother, stepping to one side, brought her straightened forearm forward and jabbed her elbow backwards, catching him such a blow in the stomach that his grief, if that's what it was, turned into shock at being treated at last like a man of the world who was being paid back for what wrong he had done.

It was as near the end of the service as made little difference. Peter's voice dried up like the rest, the blow at his father's gut timed neatly to the last line. He was bent double with pain. 'You rotten old bitch!'

'Get out of my sight. You've got no right to be here, a bogger like yo'!'

The wheeled table went through doors which opened

without a sound. If a signal had been given, Peter had missed it. The coffin was out of sight, everyone disappointed that they wouldn't see it burn. Words seemed to be rattling around in his father's throat like marbles.

'Let us all behave at such a time,' the parson called.

'Not with that devil,' his grandmother shouted.

Len tried to stop him, for having insulted his ladylove. Peter admired the speed with which his father dodged the punch and slung the flower from Len's buttonhole between the seats, which so shocked Len that he stood with reddened face looking to the front.

Peter followed his father out of the chapel but on hitting daylight couldn't stop tears rolling. Clouds in the sky sent a shower of rain as he half ran down the drive. His father had gone in the other direction, but he was too blinded to change course, and didn't want to, thinking he would come back some day.

The car nearly knocked him down as it went by, before turning out of the gate, and Peter wondered whether he was more like his father or his mother.

❊　❊　❊

Where the lane went under the wide band of railway lines was more like a tunnel than a bridge. After rain the only way to avoid pools of thin black paste, caused by coal dust sifting between the beams from each passing train, was to flatten against the wall and edge forward.

Halfway under the bridge, stunned by the thunderstorm of an express, Peter felt that the train, too heavy for the wooden supports, would fall in on him. But it was no use moving, because the noise was like God, and he wondered if God had anything to say to him, expecting the

roar to subside and a voice to tell him what the future had in store.

Beyond the bridge an elderberry tree with scores of berries leaned its branches out. Dandelions as big as saucers sprouted at the top, as well as nettles and brambles. He cut a track through, staining his palms purple. The berries stank like stale tomatoes. He pulled white pith loose with his fingernails.

Climbing a wooden fence to the railway embankment showed him the streets of Radford Woodhouse. He could see the beer-off, and Cresswell's shop, where they had fruit machines, and a secret hut in the back garden where men laid bets during big races.

If he sat on the line an express would kill him, or take a leg off. He felt soot in his nose, and the bang before a big darkness swept him away. Among the houses he picked out the window of his bedroom. Granddad Len gave him funny looks, because he didn't like him living there.

If policemen were at the end of each street no one would be able to get in or out, because a wall blocked off the far end. Jack Cope stood on a box which lifted him two feet from the ground, and Arthur Clifford used one of his hands like a stirrup, so that he was able to grip the top of the wall and get them both over. When broken bottles were embedded in concrete Jack threw up his coat to muffle them, and blood poured from his hands and knees, but next time he took a hammer and flattened enough glass to make a safer passage. The cuts festered and he went to the clinic, and had dirty bandages hanging from his hands. He frightened kids by saying he was a mummy out of a tomb.

There was plenty to do in the Woodhouse, but he was glad when he left school and got a job.

✻    ✻    ✻

'Are you going out?'

He always did on Friday.

She poured tea into a white mug. He'd given his board of ten pounds and kept five for himself. 'Your clean shirt's upstairs, but I'd like you to mend that lamp in the parlour first.'

There were stains on her blouse. She had dark curly hair, not much like a grandmother. He remembered her jabbing an elbow into his father's gut at the funeral. Her dead eyes sometimes saw everything. 'Shall you do it now?'

He was the handyman. 'I'll fetch it.'

He moved Len's bike from the sideboard and put it under the parlour window, then felt for the plug, rolling the wire and carrying the lamp by its base to the kitchen table. He'd done odd jobs when his mother was alive, unblocking sinks and mending fuses. He once put a pane of glass in the window with a few ounces of putty. Nobody else could do it, so he had to. Nor did he remember learning. He just looked and looked, and after a bit of fiddling saw what had to be done. Even at work they called on him to adjust the rollers that made the jacquards.

He took down the biscuit tin of tools. First he tried a new bulb, but it wasn't that. Opening the plug, it wasn't the fuse, either. 'I don't know what I'd do without you,' she said.

He rolled the screwdriver between his fingers. 'Has Len gone out?'

[ 27 ]

She followed his thoughts. 'Queuing up for the pub to open, I expect. He's buying the place by the pint.'

A wire was loose in the plastic switch. 'Why don't you go out, then?'

'I don't feel like it.' Her laugh was bitter. 'Maybe I ought to nip in the Crown and see if I can't catch him with another woman.' His mother was looking at him through her face. She wasn't joking, because he had seen Len in the Royal Children talking to a girl young enough to be his granddaughter. 'One of these days I'll leave him,' she said, 'if I catch him at it again.'

They'd had rows since he came, and Len would have hit her if he hadn't been there. Maybe that's another reason why she had got him to live with them. It was obvious why Len didn't like him. He plugged the lamp in. 'How's that?'

She took a kettle off the fire and went into the scullery. It was time for him to wash. He felt good getting into a suit and clean shirt. Shoes were polished and his tie pressed. He put fifty pence aside each week to get some jeans and a fancy shirt. He worked and bought things, and that was how life should be. What about tomorrow? his grandma said, and he looked as if he didn't understand, whether he did or not. It wasn't so much that he didn't know as that he didn't care.

A kid shouted, when he passed under a lamppost all spruced up and smoking a fag: 'Hey up, Samson!'

June Foster near the corner beer-off said: 'Did you hear what that little sod called yer?'

'Yes, but nobody's going to cut my hair.'

She was dark and dumpy, a quart bottle cradled in her

arms like a pet cat, to take home to her dad. 'You'd better watch it, though.'

'I will.' He was glad to talk to her.

'They'll say you're a sissy.'

His laugh covered the fact that he wouldn't like that at all. 'Everybody's got long hair now. You don't have to go into the army any more.'

'It's nearly on yer collar, though, in't it?'

Her father had a reputation for knocking his wife about, but he couldn't run very fast. Not faster than Peter when he found him in the bushes by the canal with June last year. She was only fifteen. 'Hey yo', I ain't cum yet,' she said. 'Finish me off, or else!' Nor did Jacob Foster see the condom by the bush. He was too late, as he should have known by the half-smoked fag which Peter threw away before running. 'Are you going out?'

'Yes,' she said, 'but not with you. I'm off to the pictures with Jack Cope.'

Jack had thick dark hair, and everybody loved him. 'Don't let him get you on the back row, or he'll knock you up.'

'No bogger'll knock me up.'

I'd love to, though. I'll bet you would, she'd say. He put an arm around her, but she moved away. 'You know I love you, don't you?'

'You are a funny old tune,' she said.

He told it to every girl, but not without knowing he was wrong in most cases. He relied on whoever he said it to to tell him whether he was wrong or not. He was waiting for one who would inform him that he was right, and June was nowhere near the top of the list in that respect, because it wasn't her sort he was looking for, though she'd do while he waited. What he would do when it happened he wasn't sure, but he would be grateful for it as an indication as to who he loved. So unless he claimed to love every girl he met, he had no hope of getting on any list for a real alteration in his life.

While he waited there was plenty of work at the factory, so he always had money to pay his board, last him through the weekend, and buy a few fags. You didn't need much at eighteen except a suit and a pair of overalls, though he also wanted a portable radio and a record player, not to mention a watch and a motorbike.

Jack Cope said he could have a radio any time for a fiver, but it would be nicked, and Peter didn't want the coppers on his back. Radford Woodhouse was a den of thieves, Len said, and Peter knew he was right, as he got to the bridge and took a bus into town.

❊   ❊   ❊

An old lady wearing a funny-looking birdcage hat fell with a bang on the pavement. A strong wind took her bulging handbag along the street. Outside the factory gate, Peter was sending a sack of alum up to the second floor on the hoist, and the flash of her white face alerted him. It was eleven o'clock, the taste of coffee still in his mouth.

The warm February day made him think spring was here, after the freeze-up. He worked with his cap off, ginger hair held back with a piece of string. The gaffer didn't like long hair, though Peter wasn't the only one, so he would have to lump it. Len didn't like it, either, but he knew what he could do. He didn't know whether he liked it himself, but he'd let it grow when Nancy Ecob asked him to. He wasn't going out with her any more, but he didn't want the bother of making up his mind to get it cut, especially since Len would think he'd done it for his sake.

He swung down the rope onto the pavement, and one look at her face told him all was not well. A man and woman walking up the street spared a glance, then went on, and he didn't think till afterwards what sods they were. He ran into the gateway and shouted to George in the side office: 'Dial 999 for an ambulance. An old woman's fell down.'

'None of your bleddy skylarkin'.' George went back to his newspaper. Peter and Sam Malkin once tricked him into phoning a taxi for nothing.

Peter ran inside, and the middle pages fluttered to the floor. 'If you don't get an ambulance she'll soon be dead.'

On his way out of the gate he picked up two clean sacks without thinking, though he reckoned later that he must have had something in his mind, because who ever did anything without thought, no matter how quick you acted? The old woman was as light as a feather, and must have been seventy. Looking into her face he couldn't tell whether she was dead or not. He hadn't seen anybody dead since his mother, and she had been only half this woman's age.

Open lips showed false teeth, and there was dribble on her chin. 'Come on, duck, you'll be all right. An amb'lance is coming, and they'll see to yer.' Later he couldn't remember what he said. It was easy to straighten her, so maybe she wasn't all that dead yet.

The pavement was hard, and he folded a sack into a pillow and laid it under her head. Making sure she was straight, and getting the hands down by her side, he spread the other sack over her like a blanket.

'You'll gerra bleddy medal for that,' Sam Malkin shouted from the door, but he wasn't listening, heard it while chasing after her leather handbag up the street. He put her hat by her side, and drew the strands of grey hair from her face. It wouldn't be good if she opened her eyes and couldn't see that the handbag was safe. She looked too peaceful to worry, and he wanted to laugh, but knew he should cry.

The rope of the hoist hung from the wooden arm of the loading bay, a wind wafting it to and fro. George stood at the gate like a sentry, too much of an old hand to leave his post. But he looked up and down the street as if he regretted not having done what Peter had done.

The police arrived, then an ambulance. Peter told the copper what had happened, and the copper looked at him as if he'd tried to nick the woman's purse. He even wrote down his name and address. At least they didn't search him. He went back to stacking sacks brought in by another lorry.

* * *

'An old woman died on the street today.'

She set his plate of sausages and potatoes on the table. 'Who was that, then?'

'Outside the factory.'

'I wonder why.'

'I don't know. She just died. Maybe she lived in one of them new houses at the back. I helped her, but it did no good.'

She stroked her hair by the mirror. 'It never does if it's the heart.'

[ 33 ]

'I helped her, but I don't know what it was.'

'It's allus summat,' Len said.

'She'd been shopping, I suppose.' He stretched towards the fire. On Tuesday there was nothing to do, but Len said:

'Are you going out, then?' Getting no answer, he took up the newspaper. He couldn't read, so it didn't take him long to look at the pictures. 'I expect you'll be leaving us soon, won't you?'

It was the first thing he'd heard.

Len settled himself at the fender. 'Young lads take off and leave home, sooner or later.'

'He'll go when he's ready,' his grandma said.

Len had lived at home till he was forty. Then he got married. Five years later his wife died. Peter could never understand why his grandma had let him move in with her.

'So you aren't off out, then?' His laugh wasn't very nice. 'Don't the girls love you? When I was a lad I was never in. I had to get out of the old man's way, for a start. He was a bogger to us. You could never say owt to him. He'd never listen, because his opinion was the only one as mattered. He was a mean owd bogger, as well. I don't think he ever gave me as much as a penny in his whole life. He counted every shilling as two pints of ale.'

Len went out to fill the bucket at the coal shed. Grandma's eyes sparkled with fury. 'He's just the same,' she spat out. 'Exactly the bleddy same. I wish he'd fill his sack and tek all his tranklements with him!'

He wondered how they'd got together if that was the case. Len was over sixty but was so big and vigorous that he looked fifty, whereas his grandma was sixty and you could tell. Len came back with the coal and took a quart bottle of Shipstone's best from the cupboard. He didn't offer any, having decided not to open his mouth any more except to pour beer into it.

Things had got worse between them since he came into the house, and he thought it might be because he called Len's woman grandma. Her name was Alice, and Len used it more than necessary to hint that Peter should do the same. Len didn't like to think he was knocking on with a grandmother. He fancied himself with younger women. Grandma got onto him about this, and drove him half mad, though it never did any good. Peter learned to stop calling him granddad, which was easy as soon as he realised who he was.

*　*　*

He was taking a tray of samples up to the glassed-off lab just before knocking-off time, when he met Bill Smithson, who told him he was wanted in the main office.

This is the push for sure, but he never slacked more than the others, so why him and nobody else? The machines had been going full blast for a fortnight, and Miss Tyndall in the office said plenty of orders were coming in. It didn't make sense.

A corridor led to that part of the factory smelling of furniture polish instead of paste from the jacquard section, which stank of shit. A copy of Factory Regulations by the office door had been used as a holiday camp by the flies. Whatever happened, he would get another job, because he could imagine Len's jeering if he didn't. He banged the door as if his bulbous conk was embedded in it.

Skirbeck had taken the firm over after marrying the

boss's daughter. They met at the university, and he was a timid young bloke when first brought round the factory, but now, in his mid-thirties, his short curly hair and heavy face made him seem as if born to the owner's boots. Because the place couldn't do without him any more he even felt free to cheek the old man on his weekly visit.

'Are you Granby?'

'That's right.'

'What's your first name?'

The woman sitting in the other chair wasn't his wife, and that was a fact. On second thoughts she was older than thirty, because she had grey in her hair. Her open coat showed a white jersey and a string of beads. She had a ring on her finger and smoked a cigarette, and her crossed legs in dark stockings were of a shape he'd only seen before on the pictures.

'Can't you answer?' Skirbeck said.

'Me?'

The phone rang, and he hoped it was an order for more jacquards. 'I'll call them in the morning.' Skirbeck turned back to Peter. 'This is Mrs Farnsfield. She heard about you helping her mother the other week.'

'The police told me how good you were,' she said.

He didn't like being reminded. People might think he had been soft. 'Oh well, she fell down.'

'I know. But it was very good, what you did.'

Skirbeck smiled, as if the whole thing was a bit of a joke. Peter put his weight on the other leg. It was better than getting the push.

'I thought I'd like to thank you,' she said.

Not knowing what to say, he could only feel good about what he had done, even though he hadn't thought about it. For days afterwards it had been on his mind that he had acted right and thought about every move. He felt he should thank her for thanking him. To say that he would have done it for anybody didn't seem right. Her smile suggested that his modest silence was expected. 'Where do you live?'

'Up Woodhouse.'

'Radford Woodhouse.' Skirbeck rolled a yellow pencil between his palms. 'A rough area,' he added, as if frightened of the place.

He wanted to get back to his own department, where they would be wondering what he had been called in for. 'It's not all that rough.'

'Anyway, I want to thank you.' She opened her handbag and took out an envelope. 'And to give you this. If ever you need help from me, you've only to let me know.' She put on her gloves and stood up. 'I'll remember who you are.'

Did she think he'd done it to get a reward? It served him right for giving the copper his name. But he had to. They never could mind their own business. He tried not to laugh at the idea that she would ever be able to help him, because there was something serious and hard about her when the features set and she stopped smiling. Perhaps she was still hurt that her old ma had died.

When the bell sounded for knocking-off time he took the envelope and slid it into his pocket, as if it had to be got quickly out of sight. It was hardly possible to say thank you, but when Skirbeck looked at him, he did, meaning to throw the envelope away as soon as he got into the street.

A black dog lolloped over the road, just missed by a bus
going the other way. Dogs have more lives than cats. It
pissed in the gutter, not knowing that it had nearly died.
Wagging its tail, it went up a side street by the cinema.

He climbed to the top deck for a fag, though he hardly
smoked in the week, unfolded the blue letter paper, and
saw a five-pound note. 'Dear Mr. Granby'—he'd never
been called that before—'the police told me how good you
were to my mother when she collapsed on the street, and
I'd like you to have the enclosed as a token of my thanks.'
Her name was Eileen Farnsfield, and the embossed letters
told him she lived in the posh area of Mapperley, and had
a telephone. He screwed the letter up and rolled it under
a seat.

The fiver crinkled in his pocket, a big addition to what
he had already saved, but it seemed special because it was
something he hadn't earned, and not to be frittered away
on fags or ale. The third of a mile down the lane could
seem like forever in bitter weather, but he did it in ten
minutes. Money you hadn't earned was more of a problem
than cash that made up your wages. He used to look in
shop windows for at least half an hour before spending
what coppers his mother gave him.

The five-note stayed a few weeks in his pocket, till
Jack Cope, leaning against a lamppost, held up a natty
little cream-coloured wireless with red knobs. 'Ain't it a
beauty?' He handed it to Peter. 'Go on, have a go.'

He heard the music of a pop group. 'How much do you
want for it?'

He snatched it away. 'Ten quid.'

He held the note. 'I've only got five.'

'That'll do.'

The radio was in his hand, and the money gone, but he'd got what he'd been wanting for years. All the same, he felt it had come too easily.

'Cum on, duck,' Jack called. 'We've got sum munny so we can go downtown now.'

June Foster was halfway along the street, but Jack's sharp eyes hadn't been dulled by a day's work. Or it was a put-up job. 'You've gorra bargain,' he said. 'I've done yer a favour, and don't forget it. It's one o' them transistors.'

He walked into the house with the radio still playing.

'Where did you nick that?' Len said.

'I've never nicked anything in my life.'

'It's nicked, though.'

'I gave five quid for it.'

'More fool you.' He slopped into his supper of spuds, meat and greens as if the Bomb was going to drop in two minutes instead of four. The length of fat that hung from his mouth like a snake didn't stand a chance. Peter had never told about the woman giving him the five-pound note, for fear he wouldn't be believed. 'You'd better go upstairs if you're going to listen to that monkey music.'

There was a telly on the dresser, probably left over from the Battle of Hastings, but they only watched horse racing. Grandma was right. Len gets more like his own father every day. 'It ain't monkey music.'

Len's face reddened, even below the roots of his white hair. 'Don't tell me what's monkey music and what ain't.'

He must be a monkey if he was so sure. Because his dad had been a bastard to him he couldn't be quite as much of an absolute bastard to anybody else. He would only have been that much of a bastard if his dad hadn't bullied him so much, but his dad, being the bastard he was, had bullied him. Nevertheless, he knew that Len had more chance of being a bastard with somebody pushing nineteen than with a chap of twenty-five who might when up against it turn out to be a bigger bastard even than Len. But if the call came, though not quite as big as Len, he felt able to look after himself due to nearly four years in a factory. He could tell by the look in Len's eyes that Len knew it, though it would be a shame to get blood over his grandma's sofa. 'What tunes do you like, then?'

'Eh? Well, I dunno.'

He switched the wavelength over a garble of music and speech. 'You get whatever you want.'

Len thought about it. 'I like "In a Persian Market." '

He smiled, but you never knew whether he was trying to be funny, and that was why his grandma hated him, though she wouldn't get out of his clutches because she looked after him too well. 'Never heard of it.'

'Lovely piece o' music.' He whistled some while buffing up his shoes. Peter supposed he'd had to polish his dad's boots twice a week, and if they didn't shine enough he got kicked across the room. When he was sure Len was going to tell him this, he said: 'You off out, then?'

'Just to t' top o' road. Alice'll be back soon. She's gone to get some ham for your tea.'

The radio had a funny little earphone, and he listened in on the bus, houses to one side and the grey walls of the tobacco warehouse on the other. He clocked in five minutes early, and Ted Croxley who worked the presses said: 'That's a nice wireless. How much do you want?'

'Ten quid.'

He opened the back, took out the batteries and replaced them. 'I'll give you seven.'

'Piss off.'

'Eight, then.'

'All right.'

'I'll have the money by this afternoon.'

Richer by three quid, he could buy another wireless from Jack and make three more, maybe four or five. After such buying and selling he might be able to afford a topcoat from the Coop, feeling more than nesh these days compared to when he was twelve and went out in any weather with neither coat nor jersey. He wasn't so daft as to expect Jack to have a stall of radios on the pavement, but he was disappointed at not seeing him there at all.

The street was quiet, not even a few kids playing marbles on the cobblestones. A strong smell of soot came from coal fires, as if everyone was burning the last stocks of winter.

Len shook as if he'd got a fever. 'I've been waiting for yo'.'

Peter took his coat off. The light dazzled him. 'Have you?'

His grandmother sat white-faced at the table. No food was ready, and none had been set for Len, either. Something must be wrong, but at least nobody seemed to have died.

Len looked as if about to have a stroke, veins at his temples working like water wings. 'You're not coming back 'ere,' he shouted. 'Yer can pack up and gerrout.'

'Oh shurrup, will yer?' his grandma said.

Peter turned to her. 'What's up with him?'

'The police came.'

Len stood above him like a rock about to fall in an avalanche. A few words from the cops had turned his insides to jelly.

'They got Jack Cope, and found his house full of stuff. Jack hadn't nicked it. His dad and his brother Denzil had done it. They must have knocked Jack about a bit at the cop shop, because he admitted selling some stuff to lads in the street. They came here and had a look around. I was just putting things straight when Len came in, and he's upset.'

It was as if the Invisible Man had fired a catapult at Len and hit him right in the gullet. When he jumped, Peter stepped aside, ready to fight for his life. 'Upset?' Len shouted, 'Upset? I'll kill him!'

Peter's heart was banging. 'Try it.'

'I've never done owt in my life. Never. Not a thing. And now at my age the police come and search the house looking for that rotten little tinpot monkey music radio. I allus towd yer to keep away from that Cope lot. So now I'm telling yer to get out of my house.'

'It's my house,' his grandma said. 'I own it, and it's in my name.'

'But I live in it,' Len bawled.

'You're a fucking bigmouth,' Peter said.

His head rang against the lintel, and it took a second to realise that Len had punched him. If his grandma hadn't screamed, maybe he would have done nothing, but her shriek showed his mother's face when she was lying on the settee and moaning that he should run and phone the doctor.

Unable to imagine a young lad hitting an older man, Len hadn't expected the clenched fist. He hit the sideboard on his backward stumble, and the mirror dropped from the wall and broke. The frozen leer on Len's face was more frightening than the violence, as if Peter had struck his own father with the force that his mother would have liked.

'Nobody hits me,' he shouted. He fought to say nothing more. His grandmother was a graven image, hands crossed on the table, which had no tea cloth on it, her face as ashen as Len's was flushed. He didn't want to have a fight, which would force her to go for one side or the other.

The air was clean and sweet in the yard, and he heard no noise from the house. Not that he expected anyone to call him back. They supposed he would go in on his own. He'll cool down, Len was saying. These young lads are all the same. Just like I was at his age. I'd better get some supper together for when he does come back, his grandma would say.

He called at the beer-off for a pork pie. Lottie, the young woman, must have heard about the police raid, because she was usually much friendlier. As traffic went over Radford Bridge he looked into the canal; no water, only a neat cut in the earth. Further along it had been filled in. People can't even drown themselves. A wardrobe lay on its back, and a tabby cat visible under the glow of the road lights cleaned itself. He heard the soft drop of its feet as it leapt onto the bank after a rat. Maybe a python would get them.

\* \* \*

He sat on the top deck of a bus with his legs up at the front. The further he got from home the better he felt.

Someone came on with a bundle of fish and chips, and though his stomach ached from the pork pie the smell made him hungry again.

Lights in the town centre promised comfort and warmth. He hopped off at the Coop and went through a twitchel towards Slab Square, surprised at finding the pubs so full. Because it was Monday his working clothes were clean, and he stood at the bar of the Wine Lodge and called for a pint.

Half the beer went down in one long swallow, and the rest would have gone with the same speed but he wanted to make it last. He walked to a pillar and stood there. The place was full of people who—his grandma would say—were up to no good. Their talk was so noisy he could hardly hear himself wondering where he would sleep that night.

A woman with long teeth and ginger ringlets muttered to a small man in a nicky hat wearing a smart suit with a waistcoat. The moustache seemed to be pencilled on, and his eyes shone with bad temper. The good-looking woman who held a short drink and smoked a cork-tipped cigarette seemed a bit miserable. She wore a brown costume and high-heeled shoes, and had a flimsy scarf at her neck.

The man's words made her wince, and when she said something back he put his shoe on her foot and pressed down until she was ready to cry, unable to pull away without it hurting more. Peter went close. 'You've got your foot on her shoe.'

There was malice in his expression. 'It's nowt to do wi' yo'.'

His ear was clean and neat, like everything about him.

'If you won't get your foot away,' Peter said, 'I'll drag you outside and stamp on your face.'

'I hope you know what you've done,' she said when they were alone and she bent down to rub her foot. 'Thanks, anyway. He looks after me. We had an argument. He thinks I'm cheating him.'

'He shouldn't crush your foot.'

By her talk she was not from Nottingham. 'He does worse.'

He finished his drink. 'What's your name?'

'What does it matter?'

She smelled of scent and powder. 'I just asked.'

'Iris. He's a rotter. But they all are.'

He showed his empty glass. 'Do you want another?'

'I'll have a gin.'

A few bob down the drain, but why worry? They sat at a table upstairs, and she lit another cork-tip. 'I'll just have this, then get back to work.'

He knew what she did, so didn't ask. Some women did, but most didn't. Maybe it was better than working in a factory. 'I'd go straight home after you leave here.'

The second drink made him feel easier. 'I can look after myself,' he said. She asked where he worked. 'Fetching and carrying in a factory. I live up Woodhouse, but I got chucked out tonight.' He thought talking would cheer her up, but realised he'd have to come out with something funnier than his own troubles. She thanked him for the drink, and was soon nattering to somebody else at the bar.

He walked up Mansfield Road, where a bed and breakfast sign glowed at the top of some steps. There was a counter just inside, and the place smelled damp. A fry-up was going on in the kitchen. When a thin-faced man in a worn suit came down the stairs, he asked: 'Have you got a room for tonight?'

There weren't even any carpets along the hall. 'Sorry, mate, we're full up.'

At the next place a girl showed him into a room where the stippling over the wall looked like dead bugs. He was about to hand over his money when a woman came in with a pot of flowers and said the room was let.

You'd think the Cup Final was on, or he looked as if he'd picked up the pox. Maybe he should have carried a suitcase and had a tart on his arm.

A shopping centre was being built where the old station had been. Lights winked behind the boards. It was eight o'clock but he wanted to lie down and sleep, even if only under Trent Bridge. In Slab Square, eating fish and chips in the drizzle, he remembered that if you stood by the concrete lions long enough you would see everybody in Nottingham.

Part of the copper's job was to look at him. They looked at everybody, as he would have done if he'd been one. Luckily they hadn't found Jack Cope's hot radio in the house, otherwise he'd have caught more than a glance.

The seats were wet, so he dropped the paper in a wire basket and went on towards the Castle. Clouds moved above the walls, and a courting couple passed without looking up at the moon.

He didn't have much, but at least he had his job at the factory, where he must be in the morning. Otherwise he was drifting—though a good long piss against the Castle wall might not be a bad idea so as to get pulled in and given a night's lodging in a cell. He preferred to make his way through medieval streets towards the Royal Children. If he saw Len he would treat the mean old sod to a pint so that their quarrel would blow over and they'd go home together. Optimism veered him along, but the song he whistled hardly got into its stride.

'That's the one,' somebody said.

He didn't turn round fighting, in case the police had caught up with him. It wouldn't have mattered, because someone with a house in his fist hit the back of his head. The midnight lights of Goose Fair exploded, and rained down fragments so heavy that they pushed him into the gutter.

He fell through layers of heat and cold to the bottom of a lake, and wanted to stay there, except that his head rubbed along the washboard bed of gravel. A light blinded him, and he heard someone laughing.

Eyes were glued shut, and his mouth ached. He hit the earth so hard that the sky blocked his nostrils. Scraping the rough bricks, his other hand felt his bollocks to make sure they were still there. They had thrown him over a fence of corrugated tin, onto a heap of builder's rammel, and he wondered how long ago it was. In the sky he could see stars, and cars passed by.

The pound notes were still there, so it was hard to say why they'd done it. An ache was so big it was trying to get out of his head, but when there seemed no hope of it succeeding he stood up and leaned against the wall.

The bricks wobbled like paper. Even the coins were still in his pocket, and he stretched to see if he could reach the top of the wall, hardly feeling pain, wondering whether it wouldn't be better to stay where he was instead of looking for a room.

His body warmed the bricks. The crow of a cockerel

was a peculiar hooter, which turned into the siren of a police car bowling by to catch thieves or stop a fight at chucking-out time.

He remembered the Wine Lodge, and Iris's pimp. Gripping the top of the wall, he tried to yank himself up, but pains rocketed down to the soles of his feet, so he swore and dropped.

Street lights and the moon glowed into his den. A knot had been pushed out of a plank, and his hand went through. At the bottom it was loose, and he had more strength to work horizontally than vertically, so that in spite of the head pain he pushed with his shoulder until two panels swung loose like an inn sign.

A motorist must have thought that the nightmare of his life was about to come true when he staggered across the pavement and stopped just short of the road. Up the hill was the General Hospital, but he felt as if he'd committed a crime by being injured, and that the police would nail him for it. His impulse was to go back to the rammel and hide. The hole in the back of his head was wet, and not from rain.

The light of a telephone box made it seem close, but he'd never get to it. He shook his eyes open. His body didn't want to do what it was told, so what bloody good was it? A couple came by. 'They can't tek it, these days,' the man said. 'They get pissed on pop music, and owt else paralyses 'em.'

The phone box was glued shut, but his fingers curled into the lip and pulled enough of a gap to get his foot in. He read the book and found the number. 'Mrs Farnsfield?' It was hard to drill his words into a straight line. 'This is Peter Granby—from the jacquard factory.'

'Who?' When they were kids they'd phone people and ask them to whistle because they were telephone men and wanted to test the line. If anybody whistled—and they sometimes did—they would ask if they were interested in half a ton of birdseed going *cheep.* Then they ran away laughing. 'Oh, what do you want?'

He couldn't say, exactly. 'I was hit on the head. I think somebody's killed me!'

She laughed. 'It's eleven o'clock. Where are you?'

'In a phone box at the bottom of Postern Street. I can't go anywhere.'

'Can you get a taxi?'

The driver would say he was drunk and not take him. He tried to make her think he was laughing. 'It don't matter, then.'

The line was quiet, and when he fell he thought, with anxiety and regret: 'I won't be able to go to work in the morning.'

# PART TWO

*A* PICTURE showed green trees and people with umbrellas, done in a kind of stippling. 'We thought you'd got concussion, among other things.' A thin white radiator stood by the door. 'Where do your parents live?'

The walls were beige, and there was moulding around the ceiling. 'My mother's dead, and my father's vanished.'

She sat by the bed and lit a cigarette. 'You were living somewhere, though.'

A mauve sweater made a rise over her breasts, and her nails were varnished. Keep your eyes to yourself. 'At my grandmother's. They chucked me out.'

'Hell!'

She looked paler than before, but maybe she was older than thirty. First he saw more grey, then he saw less. 'I've got some money. I'll find a place. I've got to go to work, though.'

'Not in this state you don't. I'll let them know what happened.' While she'd gone he recalled as much of the story as he had energy for, then drifted into sleep.

She held a tray of bread and butter, coffee in a blue and white pot, a mug the same colour. 'What did happen, anyway?'

The pink and white striped pyjamas intensified his headache. He had no shoes, but then, he wouldn't have, would he? He told her about the radio bought from Jack Cope, the argument with Len, and his visit to the pub.

'Is that all?'

He'd never felt so dazed, but he ate. 'I can't remember anything else.'

'I mean, you're not in trouble with the police?'

'No. I never have been.'

'That's a blessing. I phoned the factory. You'll be all right for a day or two.'

'How did I get here?'

A slight wrinkle at her eyes made him glad that she thought it was funny. 'Don't you remember?'

'Some of it.'

'A policeman thought I was kidnapping you. He also thought you were drunk, in spite of the blood. But he helped me to shoehorn you into the car. The doctor next door popped in when I phoned.'

He wondered how you could get up and go to work in winter from a room that wasn't even cold. 'I can't believe where I am.'

'Rest some more,' she said. 'I must go and talk to my cleaning woman.'

Staring at the ceiling, floating back and forth over the last twenty-four hours, he wanted to disappear, from shame at having phoned a woman he'd only seen for a few minutes. Such cheek made it even stranger that she had rescued him, but he was too dizzy to think, and his clothes were nowhere to be seen, so he had to stay where he was.

There was no pisspot under the bed. Outside, a woman wearing an apron pushed a vacuum cleaner up and down a piece of carpet, the sort of flash machine that should have L plates on it. He asked where the lavatory was. 'There, duck,' she said, 'just next door.'

He emptied his guts as well, and steadied himself on getting up. The handle wouldn't flush and, not wanting to leave a stink, he took the lid off to adjust the ball cock. The arm was metal, but in spite of his grogginess he wrenched it so that the water came to a higher level. He put the lid on the cistern and pressed the lever. A full flush resulted, but his head pounded twice as much. Back in his room, the bed had been made.

When he woke again it was breakfast, as if he'd had no sleep since he was born. A bottle of orange juice stood by his bed, and a newspaper called the *Guardian*. In the factory they'd been at work an hour already, and he'd surely get the sack if he went back now. He wondered what Len and his grandma were thinking, and hated the idea of having to ask if he could live there again.

She wore slacks, and a white blouse fastened with a purple brooch, an outfit which made her look taller. 'How are you this morning?'

'My headache's gone.'

'Until you try to walk, I suppose.'

'I'll use the bus.'

'You had a big bang.'

He felt it, and winced. 'Can I have my clothes?'

'Mrs Adkin put them in the machine.'

Now he couldn't show the bloodstains off at work and

boast how he'd been in a fight. 'Thanks.'

'Put this on and come into the kitchen for breakfast.'

'Whose dressing gown is it?'

She sipped her coffee. 'My husband's.'

The built-in stove had two silver lids, and facing him was a dresser with all kinds of pots on it. 'Is he at work?'

'He died a couple of years ago.'

Two fried eggs seemed as big a breakfast as even a condemned man would need. 'First your husband,' he said, 'and then your mother. I'm sorry.' The side of her lips were thinner than in the middle, and lifted slightly in an expression between humour and pain. 'Was it a car crash?'

'He had Hodgkin's disease. Do you know what that is?'

'A sort of cancer?'

'Right.'

The pot of tea was all for himself, with a large mug. 'You had a lot to put up with. I'm sorry I phoned you the other night. I can't think why I bothered you.'

She looked as if she might not altogether know why, either. Her face broke its repose and she said: 'My husband was an architect.'

And I'm wearing his pyjamas and dressing gown. He felt momentarily peculiar. You'd have thought she'd have thrown them away, but he connected the fact that she hadn't with her rescue of him from the phone box.

When she refilled her cup he wondered how she could drink black coffee with no sugar. 'He always wanted to be a painter—an artist—but he made such a good living as an architect that it was impossible to give it up. Maybe if he had he'd have lived longer. But we were poor at the beginning, and he couldn't face going back to that.'

'Perhaps he'd have died sooner.' He spread butter and marmalade thickly on his toast. She only wants me to listen, he thought, so I'd better shut up.

'He had a studio built for himself, and said he would paint in his spare time. Whenever I went over to see how he was I found him asleep on the couch.'

'He must have been tired. I like that painting in the room I slept in.'

'He did that when he was a student.'

Breakfast over, he asked for his clothes, not caring to put her out any more. While dressing, he saw himself in the mirror, and decided to get a haircut. He wanted to say goodbye, and was shown into a large square room called the lounge, with a high ceiling and French windows along one side looking over a well-manicured garden. She pointed out the studio-hut at the end.

'Let me show you the house.'

The staircase went up from the hall, into a space as big as his grandma's parlour. She opened all the bedrooms except the one that was hers. Each of the two bathrooms was larger than the room he had slept in. She was talking to him and showing him things and he wondered why, because hadn't she done enough already?

A pendulum clock said it was eleven. He sat on the settee, and Mrs Adkin brought in more coffee, and biscuits which only he ate. He wanted to get going, but not so abruptly as to show that he had no manners. She asked if he liked working in the factory.

'It's all right.' At home they might be silent for hours, but here it seemed wrong, though it was as much her fault as his. 'I mean, you've got to work, ain't you?'

She played with the beads around her neck. 'Would

you work somewhere else, if you had the option?'

He took cigarettes from his pocket, but the first was broken and wouldn't draw. 'Depends what it is.'

She opened a silver-topped box. 'Have one of these. I'm asking for a reason.'

There was an intense light in her blue-grey eyes that he could hardly meet. At work they played at staring each other out, and he nearly always won. With women it was easy, because June Foster looked away in five seconds.

'I need somebody to do odd jobs about the place. Not only here. My husband bought six bungalows at Ingoldness on the coast, and they're let to holiday-makers in the summer. He thought they'd help to provide an income when he gave up work and took to painting. So now I'm lumbered with them, and things often go wrong and need to be fixed. Mr Skirbeck told me you did odd jobs for them. And you mended the toilet yesterday, didn't you? Mrs Adkin said it was going again, so it must have been you.'

He felt stupid at not having come right out with it. 'I fixed your lavatory.' 'Oh, thanks.' 'Any time.' 'Thanks again.' 'One good turn deserves another.'

'You'll be a sort of handyman,' she said, 'and caretaker for when I have to go away. The house was broken into last year.'

'What about in the night?'

'You can live in the studio-hut. It'll solve your accommodation problem, won't it?'

Here was a silence he couldn't fill, but she'd asked a question, and he nodded.

'I'll pay you,' she said, 'a bit less than what you earn at the factory, because of the living-in. You'll be available during the normal hours, that's all.'

He couldn't think of a good reason to say no. Days seemed to go by instead of seconds. He had no option but to think about the most agreeable kind of forceput. But it was a forceput all the same.

'Well?'

'Thanks for the job. What do I do now?'—as if he expected a screwdriver and paintbrush to be put into his hand. Trying not to laugh, he touched the scab of dried blood on the back of his head, and the ache convinced him that what few brains he had were open to inspection.

'Do you have any clothes?'

'A suit I can fetch.'

'Take three days to get yourself organised. Then we'll see. You're still a bit pale.'

No use lying. 'You can say that again.'

'My name's Eileen, by the way.'

He stood up. 'I know already.'

*　*　*

She must be lonely, but she was good-looking and well-off, so it was hard to understand. He could do nothing except mull on his luck, while sitting on the bus with a suitcase she'd lent him.

Standing by the door while he packed, his grandma said she'd been worried to death. He shouldn't tek any notice of Len, who had quietened down and said he could come back whenever he liked. That kind of argy-bargy happens in all families.

He was leaving because he'd got a living-in job as caretaker and handyman, with a woman up Mapperley. 'I'll be well looked after.'

'And who is she?' she wanted to know. 'Does she have a husband? You'd better be careful. I've heard them stories before.'

'I'll look after myself. I'll be nineteen in a month. It's better than being in a factory.'

She didn't believe him, but it was a long time since she had worked in one. Even Len only washed up in the canteen. 'I'll call and see you now and again.'

The street was empty, kids at school and everybody else at work. Otherwise they were in their houses, except Mrs Foster, who, in spite of her cut lip, called out as he went by, 'Are you off on yer 'olidays then, Peter?'

He tapped his suitcase. 'I hope so.'

He was going to work, and that was a fact. Nothing could ever be for nothing.

A window of the studio was broken, so he fixed it with glass and putty. He dragged everything out and swept the concrete floor, filled three vacuum bags with dust. Behind a pile of canvasses he found a shotgun and a belt of cartridges, though the webbing was mildewed. Eileen told him that the gun had been given to her husband Fred by an old farmer when they'd had a cottage in the country. Fred used to joke about how it might come in handy after the Bomb went off and he'd need to stop people looting the house—if it was still standing. The gun was unsafe, she said, but Peter tightened the screws, cleaned and polished it, though couldn't eliminate all the rust on the barrels.

When he had washed the walls, put curtains at the windows, and laid some old carpet down, he hung the gun from two hooks between the beams as a decoration. He cleaned the single bed and the chair, and scrubbed the table, looking at his abode with pride, amazed that he had it to himself.

He got the motor mower working, but the grass on the lawn was waiting for spring. In the cellar was a work-bench, and half-made-up models of streets and houses. He sorted tools and nails and screws, fixed lights and replaced lino. He hammered in new shelves to store maga-zines, wondering why she hadn't chucked 'em away. The nozzle of the vacuum cleaner sucked dust and cobwebs out of all corners.

While having a quiet smoke, he twitched at footsteps on the stairs, as if afraid of getting the sack. She laughed at his expression. 'I've been walking outside the house, and there's a grate blocked up with leaves, under one of the bushes. Will you have a look at them?'

He cleaned up the mulch, and reached under the water to scoop out the sedimental slop. Car wheels crunched on the gravel as she went out. Her perfume was still with him, seemed even to be on his lips. For his nineteenth birthday she bought him a watch. 'Now you'll know what time it is.'

Two days later he took it to her and she showed him how to wind it. He could see her wondering how she could have set anyone on who was so stupid. He'd seen watches wound before, but the possibility of it being nec-essary in his case had shut itself out because there were other things in his mind. The factory had gone. His grand-mother and Len were wiped out. His split head was healed.

Walking in town after his haircut, he even passed June Foster without noticing her. 'Hey,' she shouted from halfway down Birdcage Walk, 'don't yer know me then, stuck-up!'

The panmouth was unmistakable, yet welcome all the same. She was thinner, and wore a smart navy blue skirt and jacket. When he asked about Jack she said: 'He's in one o' them detention centres. He writes to me now and again. I don't suppose they'll change him much.'

Nor did he. 'You look nice,' he told her.

'So do you.' His new suit had become his old suit, but it seemed new enough to her. She leaned on one foot. 'Don't you like Woodhouse, these days?'

'I don't get much time.'

The chimes of Little John bonked out over Slab Square. 'You'll have to find it then, won't yer?'

'If I can.' He watched her walk to the church, then turn right towards the Eight Bells.

He made breakfast on a Baby Belling hotplate, but Mrs Adkin either took him a dinner at one o'clock or he was free to have it in the kitchen. There was more chance of seeing Eileen there, but she sat in the lounge eating salad and brown bread, which he thought was hardly enough to feed a rabbit.

Mrs Adkin was a widow whose four kids had flitted. She came in four hours a day and ran the place. Peter took care of the rest. He avoided the living part of the house unless there was something to do, much as he had steered clear of the factory offices. He went in by the kitchen, and was crossing the hall to get into the cellar workshop when Eileen came in by the front door with the shopping. 'You seem to be avoiding me these days.'

He wondered if she was mocking him, and said he was

going down the cellar to get a three-point plug for the electric fire in the studio.

'Are you warm enough out there?'

He was. 'But I like to have everything working.'

'All nice and shipshape, eh?' She took off her white blanket-type coat and woollen hat. 'Come into the lounge, and we'll have some coffee.'

When they sat down she said: 'How would you like to take driving lessons?'

He held his mug steady. 'I'd like it.'

'I'll fix you up with three lessons a week for a month. That should be enough to get someone like you through your test.'

He felt her gladness at his having made such an impression, and because it was one of his most important moments he did something which he realised was stupid. But he couldn't help it. He reached out to shake hands on the deal, and when she took it, in a jokey manner, he pressed hers so firmly that she drew back. But she had let it rest a few seconds before he put the pressure on. 'That's wonderful,' he said, feeling himself the colour of blood. 'Thanks, Eileen.'

A flicker of something—he couldn't tell what—flashed over her eyes, a motion which he knew had also been registered on the thin, downcurving lips. 'I sometimes get sick of driving.'

'You mean I'll be able to drive the Rover?'

In spite of her laugh there was misery behind her face, though he couldn't tell why. 'Unless I change it for something else.'

He clipped grass around the rose bushes, mindlessly going along each border because he gloried in the idea of driving a car. His hands weren't fit for less soothing work, and it nagged him that he couldn't do anything in return for her big favour. He scooped up weeds and cuttings, put them in a barrow, squashed them down with his boot, and took them to the compost heap.

Three early roses were about to spread their petals, so he clipped them, and pulled off thorns with his fingernails so that she wouldn't prick herself. Nobody was in. But what would he say if she sprang out of a room and asked what he was doing? The place felt dead. I thought I would drop the odd rose here and there. How can the house be dead when I'm in it, she would say. If that's your opinion of the house you'd better get back to where you came from. I'm sure it's a lot livelier there. Skirbeck says it was, didn't he?

Bay windows looked over the front, curtains draped to either side. Half-open doors of the sliding wardrobe showed dresses like the coloured spines of tall books, and he wanted to pull a few out to guess how she would look in them. The red roses enlivened the counterpane which covered her bed like a field of snow—like blood that's fallen from the ceiling, as if there's a body dripping to death in the attic, though he knew there wasn't because he'd been through every beam on getting to know the house.

Opposite the dressing table was a writing desk, and a small padded chair which would break if he sat on it. She wrote to Penny that she was thinking of getting a dog, and though he would be scorched to blindness at reading her private words, his sight was fixed by her writing.

'I didn't tell you, but I picked up this young man to live in Fred's old studio. He's a kind of handyman cum guardian, and very quiet, but useful in all sorts of ways. No, not *that*. And I did pick him up, literally, because he'd been injured in a fight. Funnily enough, he phoned me because I'd met him before. When my mother collapsed on the street he was as gentle as a nurse, and tried to make her comfortable. He's nice, really, and I'm slowly civilising him. Not that that's my aim in life, I'm far too busy, but it seems to be happening.'

No sign of a car coming into the drive; he wanted to run as far from the house as he could get and never come back. The dream of driving swept out of his mind. Did she think he was uncivilised? He took the roses back to the garden, wondering why he hadn't ripped the letter up and scattered that on her bed.

He dug a hole and buried them because it was impossible to put them back on their stalks. Luckily there were a few more, and he hoped she wouldn't notice, but next morning she said: 'The garden looks a lot neater, but what happened to those roses?'

'I cut them by mistake. They weren't good enough.'

Her eyebrows lifted. 'Took them to your girlfriend, I suppose?'

He said nothing. Let her tell her pals she hadn't civilised him.

'They'll grow back, I expect. Your first lesson's at two this afternoon.' She walked away; no invitation to coffee this morning.

❊   ❊   ❊

After lesson one he thought he could take the test any time and pass. At the third session the bloody Imp wouldn't do anything right. But soon he was driving around the streets as if born at the wheel, and asked Eileen to cancel the last three lessons. She had paid for the job lot in advance, though, and kept him at it.

On their way back from the test centre she was able to say: 'You passed first time!'

He was glad to surprise her but sorry at her low expectations.

'To celebrate,' she went on, 'you must have a meal with me tonight.'

He liked the idea of going to a restaurant.

'I'll make you something special.'

He'd rather call on his grandma and Len in the car, then pick up June Foster and take her to the Wine Lodge. But at seven, wearing his suit and tie, he walked through a smell of roses and honeysuckle to the house.

The smooth dark skirt went down to her feet. He was aware of how tall she was, though a few inches shorter than him. The bottle of wine had a metal-covered cork and a wire cage over the top, and two shallow glasses lay on the low table.

He knew he made a good impression because she told him to open the champagne, and he didn't flinch when the cork hit the ceiling like a bullet and came down on a plant in the corner. 'It's the only test I ever passed.'

'Congratulations, then. I wasn't sure whether you'd get through or not, but I hoped you would.'

'I just did it,' he said. 'I didn't want to think about it, in case I got nervous.'

She observed him, as if not sure that he was speaking truly. 'Sounds very sensible. But as you get older it gets less and less possible.'

He laughed. 'Not with me, it won't.'

'Well, you never know.'

The champagne got up his nose and made his eyes feel tight. 'I am like I am. I don't suppose I'll alter.' She made no sense in thinking he ought to. Her low-cut white blouse showed the parting of her breasts, and he asked what the stone was in her brooch so that she wouldn't think he was staring.

'Tourmaline.'

'I've never seen one before.'

'My husband gave it to me.'

He refilled their glasses. 'It's nice.'

He didn't care if she was mocking him. Passing the test had made him feel good. 'This champagne's better than a pint of jollop from the beer-off!'

'I should think so.'

He'd meant it as a joke. Two places were set at the shining table, and she told him to light the candle. While she was in the kitchen he worked the lighter embedded in a stone that wouldn't fit easily in any pocket. The glow shook towards the ceiling, and she stood in the doorway to look at the effect. 'Do you like minestrone?'

'It's my favourite.' It was like stew, except that there was no meat.

'There's a pot roast in the oven, and then a caramel custard for dessert. I hope that'll be enough.'

'Should be.'

'Now that you have your licence you'll have to be more careful. I hear that people are likely to prang just after passing their test.'

'I don't get you.'

She watched his large knuckles reddening as he put pressure on the corkscrew. 'When I passed I was over-

[ 70 ]

confident, and limped home one day with the wing bashed in. My father was furious.'

He knew how to control his strength, so there was no splash of wine. 'I'll be careful. I passed the Highway Code as well, you know.'

'I saw you reading it,' she laughed, 'walking up and down the garden. I thought you were saying your prayers!'

She put the pot roast on a platter and arranged vegetables like a garland. His right hand was behind her back, and he wondered whether she felt its nearness, and what she would do if he let it rest on her. It was too early after passing his test, and he wouldn't want her to be furious, though he was inclined to believe that she wouldn't mind.

The heat between his palm and the small of her back increased the longer he held it there. Perhaps most of it came from her body, and she wanted the gap to close.

'If you carry this in, I'll bring a few other things.'

She drank more than he did, but he let his glass rest, and enjoyed eating. 'Have you always lived here?'

'Oh, no. At first we had two grotty rooms in London. We got here by stepping stones, you might say. Fred found a good job, then he inherited property from his father. It was fairly quick once it started.'

She left half her meat, while he had a second helping. 'Be nice if everybody could live like this.'

She took a small stick from a container and picked her teeth. 'A habit I acquired in Spain. I'd like everybody to have a nice house, as well. We used to be in the Labour Party. The trouble is, there aren't enough nice houses to go round. Would you like to share the car with half a dozen others?'

[ 71 ]

He didn't have to think twice. 'No fear.'

She stood, knocking the chair. Maybe she was just tired. He followed her with the loaded tray into the kitchen. If she had been sober he would have tried, but if he made a move while she thought she was drunk she'd be bound to make a fuss, and that would be no good. And if she thought *he* was drunk that wouldn't help much either.

When she took a tub of cream out of the fridge, and reached above the range for a jug, his arm went around her waist, lips at the warm skin of her neck. He didn't know whether he wanted to slide a hand up her leg or stroke her breasts. She shuddered and turned when his hands teased her ribcase. The jug bounced from the cutting board and hit the corkwood floor. 'No,' she said, 'don't do that.'

Her eyes expressed cool surprise, yet there was an amused looseness on her lips. He felt her measuring him, trying to read him deeper than he had ever thought worthwhile. His whole life seemed to be in the balance. He wondered which way things would go, though ready for another attempt. If she didn't like it, she would say so, and wouldn't give him the push because of what the driving lessons had cost.

She eased him gently away. 'I rather think not. Let's get our dessert. Mrs Adkin can clear up the mess in the morning.'

❊   ❊   ❊

She forgot to pay him for three weeks, but he had enough cash to get fags and razor blades, which seemed the only items on which he spent money. He reminded her, and when she came back from the bank he had so much money he stopped the car outside a second-hand guitar shop on Mansfield Road and walked in like a millionaire to get one, just missing a parking ticket when he came out with it over his shoulder.

He was offered a book to learn from, but he didn't need it, tinkled tunes to the warm spring evening by the open window of the studio. A tree was sprouting buds, and in their honour he plucked a harmony which made his own tune rather than any he recognised.

Eileen kept herself busy, either bossing Mrs Adkin, or up in her room answering people who wanted to rent one of her bungalows during the summer. Otherwise she was out in the car, and he didn't get much use of it.

She'd said nothing about his pass at her, so he wouldn't try again, not being much more than an odd-job man and errand boy. There were no mates to chew the fat with like in the factory, but he was almost his own boss and could drive the car now and again, which made up for everything, if there was anything to be made up for, which there sure wasn't at those times when he lay on his bed serenading the first shining star between the two branches of the tree.

'That's nice.' She stood in the doorway. 'Don't stop.'

Her hair was tied with a ribbon and she wore slim brown slacks which, when he walked behind her, were better than any skirt. 'Come on in.'

'I will, if you'll play some more.'

'I can't, when anybody's listening.'

She sat on the chair. 'I'm not anybody, am I?'

If she was, he would play without worrying.

'I've just popped over to tell you we'll be going to Ingoldness in the morning. You drive, and I navigate.'

'Sounds fine.' He'd already had the maps out of the glove box and looked at the route. 'Would you like some coffee?'

Her eyebrows lifted in a way he thought meant neither yes nor no, but she said: 'What a good idea!'

If you wanted to make good coffee you had to use a lot. 'It's almost as good as mine,' she said. 'I'll never sleep.'

'I will, as soon as my head's on the pillow. Unless.'

'Unless?'

He tried to read her eyes. To see anything would be better than nothing, even if he made it up. And if he made it up he might be right. She wanted him to say something surprising. 'Unless I'm a tiger.'

At least he made her laugh. She leaned forward, but there was still too much space between them. 'A tiger?'

'A tiger can't get to sleep. It roams around.' If she had come to his hut, which had a bed in it and was private from the house, what did she expect? 'So I roam around in bed all night, wondering all sorts of things.'

'I wish I did. My thoughts just go in circles. I worry about absolutely nothing.'

She was getting bored, so he stood up to put his guitar away. 'I never worry.'

'I should hope not.'

'You know why?'

'No, but I should like to.'

He thought she seemed frightened, bored and worried, all at the same time. 'Because I love you.' He hadn't meant to say such a thing.

'Oh, stop it. You're only nineteen, and I'm pushing forty. It wouldn't do.'

He came close. 'Who says so?'

She laughed, but he knew he was getting somewhere, and so did she. 'I don't know, come to think of it. But it wouldn't do, all the same.'

'You might be dead tomorrow—or we both might.'

She seemed to think about it, but he was wrong again. 'Get the alarm set for six. I want us to be away by eight. Put the luggage rack on so that we can take that chest of drawers from the attic. You can have breakfast in the house. Mrs Adkin will be in at seven.'

He strummed another half-hour, before getting into her husband's pyjamas that she had let him keep.

*　*　*

More traffic was coming in than going out, which was how he liked it. Maybe it was too early, or she was nervous about his driving, but neither spoke as they crossed Trent Bridge and headed for Grantham. To him it was just another test he had to pass—not caring whether he did or didn't.

She wore a grey skirt and white long-sleeved blouse, and though her smell excited him he didn't stop looking at the road. She pulled down the spare mirror, unable to see anything but her lips. He envied that few square inches of glass.

West Bridgford was dismal after Mapperley, and he was glad to have the straight road by Radcliffe almost to himself. As if going on holiday, though he knew he wasn't, he wore a tie and his second-best suit, hair well combed after the shower. Her silence made him feel more in command, and he let an articulated lorry pass before going onto the island at Saxondale Crossing, changing gear so that his passenger would feel no jerk in their motion.

Beyond Grantham three trucks gaggled on the winding road, and since there was no hope of passing he settled down to forty and kept well back, to prove he was no madhead. When the walls and turrets of Tattershall Castle came up by the roadside, as if telling him not to go beyond, he grinned at such an idea and drove on to Conningsby. 'I want to stop,' she said, so he waited while she went to the toilet, having something to remember the place by.

After Burgh she guided him along lanes to the coast, which he'd been to once on a bus trip from school. Jack Cope dodged the teachers and took him through arcades and bingo halls, later showing him the loot. 'Yer can't cum back from Skeggy wi' nowt, can yer?' The bearded teacher walked up and down the bus: 'Where did you get all that?' 'I bought it, sir.' 'Well, hide the bloody stuff.'

Peter had been spared from reform school for another sight of the flat blue sea, this time from behind the wheel of a car with a well-dressed woman beside him.

They were chalets more than bungalows, miniature cottages that a good wind might blow away. 'I had a man on the spot to look after them, but I had to get rid of him.'

He wondered what for. Must have been letting them out on his own. Or maybe he had a go at her.

'He cheated me. Sometimes I wonder why I keep them.' She picked up a cigarette packet by the door. 'But it gives me something to do, and I more than break even. Fred liked to come here in summer. He loved this coast, even though he was from London.'

The one nearest the road was cold and smelled damp.

There was a living room with an open kitchen area, a double bedroom and a single room. 'How much does it cost?'

'Fifty pounds a week, in August.'

'Christ!'

'They pack a whole family in, so it's economical.' He noted two armchairs and four kitchen chairs, as well as a settee, a table, and a black and white TV. A sailing ship picture hung on the wall, and a plastic plant pot stood on the table. 'They'd feel uneasy if it was furnished any better. Fred worked it out. He came from that sort of family himself, though his father struck it rich during the war.'

She lit a stove, and he pulled it into the bedroom. 'Now spread sheets and towels around to let them air. I want you to do the same in every bungalow and check them for complete sets. Then look around for leaks, blockages or damage to the roofs. There's a vacuum cleaner in that cupboard, so do the places over as well. You'll soon get the idea. I'm going to see a lawyer in Skegness, and then have lunch. There's food in the car that Mrs Adkin packed.'

He felt like the Lord Mayor inspecting his parish, except that there were no people. Across the road the sea was wrinkling in. Two horses were ridden along the sand, hooves hitting the shallow water as if followed by a trail of bullets. Eileen was on the first, and he was after her. They were on their way to Scotland. Each night they found a hotel with stables, then had a good meal, laughing at their adventures, and planning the next day's stint. In bed they fucked like rabbits.

He made the first chalet perfect, as a standard for the others. It didn't seem like working for money, merely helping Eileen so that she would say how glad she was at what he'd done. He listened to pop music, hearing flashes about crises in distant places, and argy-bargy between Tories and Labour. High clouds floated over a sea without boats or smoking ships.

She was surprised he had done so much. Or was it that he'd done so little? He noticed her slacks. 'I booked into a hotel,' she said.

'I thought you was going to stay here.'

'It's a bit too bleak.' She sat in an armchair. 'But you can make up the bed for yourself in number one.'

He put the kettle on. 'You aren't worried about anything, are you?'

He was getting too personal, he saw her thinking, and decided to curb himself. 'Sometimes I wish I was,' she said. 'But no, I'm not.'

He passed the tea. 'That's one good thing, then.'

She smiled. 'You *are* funny!'

'I want to look after you.'

'You're doing all right. There's a pub down the road if you get bored this evening. I've never been there, but Fred liked it. This tea's too strong.'

He emptied half, and poured in hot water. 'I never get bored. I've brought my guitar, anyway.'

There was enough to eat and drink, radio and television, a bed, and protection from an east wind that rattled the windows. Yet he wanted more, with such urgency that there was an ache in his guts.

\*   \*   \*

A grey cloud grasped the horizon like a crab as he walked between tufts of reed grass. A haze metalled the rippling sea, sun causing it to shine. The forecast was for showers, and cold rain pummelled the windows, though the room was warm. Eileen ran in from the car.

'Sit by the stove,' he said, putting her coat on a hanger. 'You're safe here.'

'It's warm,' she said.

He made out she'd lost her way in a storm. Petrol was low and the engine was knocking. The light glowed from his window. She had to shelter, and find out where she was. It was a godsend, to be welcomed into a cosy house by this kind hermit. The tea warmed her. She wanted to know how such a young bloke came to be living in an out-of-the-way place like this. 'Safe from the rain, I mean,' he said.

She didn't hear. 'I must check all the inventories before we leave.' She didn't move, either, but stared as if wanting the rain to stop and go back to where it came from. He took half a bottle of whisky from the cupboard, but didn't drink in case she needed driving somewhere.

'I'll be warmer still,' she said, when he poured her half a tumbler. He couldn't make her out, though he tried. Maybe if he tried hard enough, and kept on trying, she would realise what he was trying to do and help him. Rain stopped, and a blade of sun illuminated the settee. 'I suppose we ought to make a start then,' he said.

She put down her drink. 'I think you're right.'

The unfamiliar urgency of her tone jarred. He didn't like being told what to do in such a voice, but the feeling didn't last. Her eyes informed him that something was wrong, or different, or right, he couldn't tell which. They looked perfectly in tune to the shape of her lips and the thinness at the corners, as if not to see something but to intimidate him beyond what he could accept. He was going to move first, but didn't want to make another mistake, and in any case she didn't care for that, was determined to do it herself, because after all he was only nineteen and it was up to her. She would feel tainted if she left it to him—as it came out later.

'I got to thinking, why shouldn't I? I wanted it, but at first I didn't want you. Had no idea of it, but then I kept on thinking, why the hell not? So when I wanted you, you weren't there. When I decided against it, you *were* there. Then when I wanted you, and you were there, that's how it was. You had to wait till I wanted you—all in my own good time. That's how it had to be before I could let it happen. I'm like that, I suppose.'

He knew well enough what to do, but not what to say, so acted on the understanding that the less said the better. On the other hand he didn't seem to be doing very much, certainly not as much as Eileen. That it was hard to keep up with her didn't mean that things were going very fast either. She made no show of fighting him off, so his attempt to be the one to make love lost direction. He might have known where to go, but she knew even more what she wanted, and how soon it was to come about.

Her kisses made him uncertain, but they were no less good for that. He knew he had to relax, as his hand was permitted to travel slowly along the warm skin of her back. The fresh whisky on her lips coated his own. He couldn't even say how it happened, and held himself from actions which were premature, concentrating on his hand under her sweater, which needed its own particular brain for undoing the hook.

He didn't know whose tears were on his cheeks, her

mouth being at so many places on his face that he wanted to laugh, though he disguised it by a catch of his breath, which it turned out to be when the hook parted and his hand slid up over her breasts. The stance was difficult because she pressed him with her legs, so that he had to steady himself. She pushed his hand away when he helped her with his belt, indicating that he stand still while she undressed him and then herself, before drawing the curtains in the bedroom.

Her breasts were larger when released, making a different person bending over him with no clothes on, an unknown woman feeding her own greed as she came down and guided him into her, not caring that she would never be the same to him again. He didn't care that she cried at such a time, as he stroked her spine and the valley between her buttocks. She stared, unseeing, went back and forth along him till he felt her come, her head moving to and fro, and crying so loud he was sure she could be heard on the road. After a while she moved again so that he couldn't help but shoot into her.

She always laughed when she had something important to say. 'I must have wanted to do that ever since I saw you.'

'So did I,' he lied.

'You've flooded me!' She wiped the mess with her knickers, and hovered over him in the dim room. He didn't want to move, and there was nothing else to say except: 'I love you. You know that, don't you?'

'I suspect you're the first one who has.'

What about your husband? But he kept quiet. She finished the whisky in her glass and put a hand behind his head, her breasts close to his lips. She came a second time, then lay on her back and let him finish.

'What about our work?' he asked after a while.

She arched her eyes. 'Yes, I am rather wearing you out. Or am I?'

He didn't know what she meant, tried to get onto her, but she wouldn't have it. 'Leave things to me.'

'If that's what you want.'

'I do.'

'All right, duck.'

'Marvellous.'

'What?'

'Talking like that.'

'Like what?' He couldn't call her anything else if that was how he felt. 'You are my owd duck, aren't yer?'

She tried to rouse him again. 'Well, maybe.'

It took longer, and there was less vigour, but he knew she came, and at the same time as he did.

'Have you?' he said, but couldn't go on.

'Have I what?'

'I mean, since your husband died?'

She took time to think, and brought in tea and biscuits on a tray. 'You shouldn't ask questions, but since you do, the answer's no, though I admit I've dwelt on it in the past few months. Not that I got all that much when he was alive.'

He felt a right to go further. 'Why did you wait so long?'

'It takes a year to get over a death. Then I was afraid. I just couldn't go out and pick somebody up in a pub. And I didn't have friends who'd serve. Anyway, I liked living on my own, when I got used to it, and I was never un-

satisfied, though it didn't seem enough since you came.'

He felt privileged, as if her attempts to explain herself proved that she loved him. The sun was angry that the curtains stopped its shining on their arses. 'What are you laughing at?' she snapped.

'Because I'm glad.'

Her underwear was back on. 'So am I,' she whispered, as if someone would hear. 'I enjoyed that.'

'It was better than a hot dinner, and that's a fact.'

She made him say it again. 'Come on, though, we have work to do.'

He sat by the door pulling at his guitar. An occasional slump of waves provided percussion when he stopped. He hadn't noticed them so clearly before. Maybe the shower after all that loving washed my ears out. He wondered who she was drinking with at the hotel in Skegness. 'I'm going back to take a bath,' she said, 'and then to bed.' He imagined her stark naked in the bath. In bed she'd have a box of chocolates, and perhaps a book. After a while the book was boring and she thought of him.

❈   ❈   ❈

Her brown felt hat was much like a man's, and he hoped she'd take it off because it interfered with visibility. She didn't care what he thought, and he didn't care what he thought, either. Nor did he care very much what she thought. He wondered how she felt about him going back a different person to when he came, but didn't ask. He didn't need to. 'I don't know what you think of me,' she said, 'but I feel a lot more relaxed.' Thank you very much. It was a winding road, and he was glad when they reached the Wolds. 'Of course, it's got to be our secret.'

'I'm not going to clatfart it from the rooftops.'

'Well, I don't suppose you'd like everybody to know you're going with someone as old as I am.'

'I love you, don't I?'

She put her hat on the seat behind. 'We'll keep it to ourselves, then.'

Unmoving clouds lay above fields and woods. It was plain that she didn't want anybody to know she was going out with somebody like him. An old woman in the back of a Ford Escort was wearing a fluffy pink hat. He swung out to overtake, and got in in good time.

'We can sleep together now and again, but we don't want to die together.'

'What do you mean?'

'Well, that was a bit too close for my liking.'

He felt like smashing them to kingdom come against the next stone-laden lorry. 'What's the matter?' she said. 'I didn't upset you, did I?'

He sensed her sarcastic smile. 'I never get upset.'

'Just as well. Keep your mind on the road.'

'It'll get run over!'

She touched his hand, and smiled. He had a bellyache from rage, but her blank expression encouraged him to keep his attention on the driving. Trees and bushes darkened the verges, and he slowed down.

'Why have you stopped?'

'I'll show you.' He opened the door and held out a hand. She pressed it, as if he deserved that much. The breeze blew her hair loose. He didn't know where the hell he was going, but when she looked back at the car he said scornfully: 'It won't run away.'

A dry ridge along the middle of the muddy path led

into a wood. A rabbit stared, and he was ready to make a grab when they got close, but it switched direction and ran off with legs kicking. It was only then that Eileen saw it, and he wondered if she needed glasses.

He hadn't been this way before, but she followed, amused and intrigued by his decisiveness. They came to a clearing by a stream covered with bluebells. A thrush swooped over the glade, and no motor noises reached them. Trees and greenery surrounded the dell of paradise.

'I thought you might like it.' He looked into her eyes but couldn't tell. The view was lovely but the ground was too wet for Adam and Eve.

'You should have brought your guitar, but thanks for showing me.' She fastened her coat. 'We must go, though. I have to get the account books ready for John Scartho in the morning.'

She led the way out and, as if to make up for wasted time, drove the car back to Nottingham herself.

❊   ❊   ❊

She was so behind with his pay that one day she handed him a cheque for a hundred pounds. 'Drive me to the bank tomorrow, and you can open an account.'

'I don't need a bank.'

'What if the studio was broken into?'

He shrugged. So he had a chequebook he hardly used. When he was in a good mood he only wanted to know that she thought well of him. Mostly he was indifferent, and got on with rewiring, reroofing, reguttering, and errands in the car. But there was plenty of spare time, and the job often seemed more of a skive than anything else.

She treated him like a stone that had rolled off the fire,

and didn't want to know him, while he craved to know her more and more. With June it had been similar the next time they met, but after that it had been all right again. Eileen must have thought that with him it was a one-off thing, and decided that he wasn't worth going on with. The worry marked his face. It was time to pack the job in. Maybe his grandma would let him board there again, and perhaps even Len had changed his tune.

His tie knot was right first time. Len would like that, as well as the fact that his hair was short. He would sweeten him with a packet of Players. Eileen knocked at the door. 'I see you're going out.'

She had chosen the wrong night. 'To see my grandma.'

Her lips were sharpened with make-up. 'I was going to ask you to come to the house.'

He had rehearsed the encounter with Len and his grandmother so often that it was too late to alter his plan. But he felt her frustration. 'I'll stay if you like.'

She looked warily around, as if to spot something she'd lost. 'No, you go. I'm busy, really.'

'Can I borrow the car?'

She used the mirror, and he wondered what she saw. He saw her undressed and bending over him, a picture he wanted to frame and carry around.

'Don't drive anyone else.'

He threaded the one-way system over the hill and down into Radford. New blocks had been built, sheets of windows reaching for the sky. The White Horse was lit up, and the station was closed. He passed the Midland pub and then the Crown, and turned down the road for Woodhouse.

He manoeuvred the car to face outwards, then decided

to be polite and knock, which was just as well because a black woman opened the door and asked what he wanted. A colour telly was installed, and he thought he'd got the wrong number, if not the wrong street. 'I've called to see Mrs Granby.'

'Oh, her? She's gone. We bought the place from her. She don't live here any more.'

There was nothing to say.

'Sit down a minute.'

The ground floor had been knocked into one room, the walls coloured flock red. 'You had a granddad as well, didn't you?' A kid of five with a snotty nose and bubbly hair played with a wooden train set. 'Do you want a cup o' tea?'

'No, thanks. Do you know where they went?'

'The neighbours told me the old man had a stroke. They took him to City Hospital, and as soon as he'd gone, the woman sold the house. Nobody knows where she is. She just got the money and ran. She left him high and dry in the hospital.' She said it as if every wife in Nottingham wouldn't mind doing the same.

The boy thrust an engine towards his face, and Peter put it on the rails, which made him so happy he came back with a wagon. 'I'm sorry to upset you,' the woman said.

'I've been away.' He ran the wooden wheels up his trousers. 'What's your name?'

'Barry,' the boy said.

'Mine's Peter.'

'Are you my uncle?'

'I expect you'll find her,' the woman said.

The old world had been pulled out of his reach, and the darkness was deeper than when his mother had died because now there was no funeral to mark it. He drove on full headlights, as if no illumination was bright enough.

In a parking place by the Hemlock Stone he wound down the window to look at the stars. He didn't want to go anywhere because he didn't know what he wanted. The fact that he wanted something made him angry. He didn't want to want anything, except to be somewhere other than where he was, and that wasn't much. If he saved some money he could make an even bigger flit than his grandmother, travel for days in a straight line to find a new life.

He had a chequebook and driving licence, and he was able to vote. He had a job of a kind, and a hutch to sleep in, but what he wanted was beyond either knowing or getting, something so big in fact that he felt impelled to play on the motorway and never come off. Maybe that was what he wanted.

Calling on his grandmother one winter, he had seen a continent of white clouds and craved to climb into them to a new country. His mother was at the end of her days, so he would get there first and find a place for her. If he saw the same clouds now he'd take Eileen. They'd be so hot for each other that neither would die of the cold.

He switched off the radio and went back through the city, and when he stopped in front of the house she was framed in the lighted door, as he'd known she would be. 'Come in, after you've locked the garage.'

He laid the keys on the table, and she poured him a drink. 'You're not driving tonight.'

He was a stone in the water.

'Did you see your grandparents?'

'They weren't in.' He topped up the glass, and swigged it. 'I drove around Wollaton, then came back.'

'All that time? Don't you have a girlfriend?'

He sat down. 'No.'

'Someone like you! I'm surprised.'

'I don't care what you think.'

She sat by him. 'Why don't you?'

'Mutual, ain't it?' She's tiddly, he thought, otherwise she can't love me.

'You haven't been with a girl tonight?'

'Do you want to smell my fingers?'

'Let's go to bed.'

He didn't want to move, but her arm was around him so he kissed her. 'I love you.'

She drew away. 'I'd like to say the same to you, but I made up my mind to stay away from you. I've been through hell waiting for you to come back.'

It didn't feel like she was telling the truth, but that could have been his fault. She lifted her glass. 'Let's drink.'

'What to?'

'Can't you decide?'

He stopped thinking, and poured more whisky. 'I don't know what to choose.'

'Bring your glass.'

She kept the overhead light on, a change from the dim bungalow. Perhaps by showing off her breasts and the light hair of her cunt she was starting to love him a bit more. 'I like to see all of you.'

'Serves me right. I don't care for too much light, especially when I'm naked. So I do what I don't like. Maybe I think it's good for me.' She stroked his hard belly, and her mouth hovered around his erection. 'But I can see you,

[ 90 ]

and that's a real pleasure. I'll never want anyone older.'

He minded such puzzling remarks less when she made them with no clothes on. Across the lower part of her stomach were faint white blemishes. His finger traced their course. 'What's them?'

'I got pregnant a couple of times, and had miscarriages. They're called stretch marks.'

He cupped her breasts, and licked each nipple. 'I love your marvellous tits.'

'Are they large enough?'

'I could eat 'em.'

She closed her eyes, and moved over him. 'Talk some more like that.'

She asked, so he couldn't, but he tried. 'Not that there's owt wrong with your lovely cunt.' He'd imagined everything in daydreams and nightdreams, how to make her come without fucking, and how to fuck her without bothering to make her come, and when he muttered this she came more quickly. 'You're learning,' she said.

'I will, if you'll let me.'

They were hungry, and the fridge was a treasure cave. His grandma's fridge was the corner shop to which she might go four times a day. There was so much food in this one, and in cupboards, that if there was suddenly no grub left in the world they would stay alive six months longer than anybody else. And if anyone tried to rob them he'd hold them off with the shotgun.

'I had no supper.' She looked at him eating. 'I kept wondering when you'd be back.'

'You needn't a worried. My grandma's gone. She sold the house and flitted. Nobody knows where.'

'I'm sure you'll find her.'

He shredded a chicken leg. Her husband had died, and then her mother, so maybe she thought his loss didn't bother him. 'Not if I know her.'

She looked as if she owned him absolutely. 'At least I've got you.'

There was nothing he could say to that, but she seemed to mean it, so he peeled her an orange.

❉　❉　❉

He would stay a night or two at the bungalows, according to how much work there was. On a changeover day—clients leaving and others coming in—he stayed to check inventories and give back deposits.

If a telly packed in and he fixed it, or if a light fitting was repaired, or a drain unblocked, he might get a quid or two pushed into his hand. He was surprised when people admitted, as they sometimes did, that what had gone wrong was due to their carelessness.

Driving there and back, Eileen's face was in the rear mirror, or the side mirror, or in the windscreen. He was as careful as if she watched from every place at once. He winked and laughed, then steadied his feelings to get back in proper contact with the road.

Because he didn't know her completely, he thought he didn't know her at all. In bed he knew everything there was to know, though he wondered why they didn't go there often. If he gave a hint, she turned cold, because she had to be the one to get him upstairs. It didn't make sense, though he wouldn't have minded, as long as it happened whenever he wanted. He tried to see a pattern, wondering if her need came at the time of the full moon, or just before her monthlies. But he couldn't figure it out, only knowing that since he thought of her so much there was no doubt about his love for her. She never said she loved him, but he didn't mind, especially when they were in bed together. Knowing that there was more to a woman than that didn't increase his knowledge about her. He thought it unnecessary that she keep herself from him, because he might not have been much the wiser if she hadn't.

Nor did it make any difference knowing all her business. He saw how she talked and joked with her accountant in a loud voice, and he could see that both he and her solicitor respected her. She introduced him as her caretaker, and he noticed their amusement.

'Mr Scartho has to know about you,' she said, 'because your wages come off my tax. Have you ever been a tax loss before, Peter?'

'I expect I was when I worked in the factory.'

She bought him a tape recorder, and he wondered if that was also a tax loss, though he took it as a gift of love rather than a tip for efficient work.

He drew tunes from the guitar, and taped a program for Eileen's birthday, but the words fitted neither him nor her, and his voice came out as flat and ignorant. A few paragraphs read from the newspaper at least sounded as if he knew something of the world. You had to be familiar with your own voice if you wanted to get on, he thought, and hearing it played back gave you a respect for it. A voice divided from the body made two of you, and by doubling your understanding you doubled your power, though if you weren't careful it could send you daft, so he turned it off and hung it on the wall by the gun.

The sea was so blue and flat that even in June it looked cold. Perhaps he should bring the gun and shoot at mallards that flew from the marshes and disputed the dunes with the gulls. He wondered what they'd be like to eat, but wouldn't hit one because they were farther away than he thought. Their amusing manoeuvres hypnotised him, and he rolled over on the sand, pretending to aim.

The sea was like an empty page waiting to be turned, and when it was, Eunice waited at the door of the bunga-low. 'Me mam's telly's gone bust,' she said. 'Can yer come and fix it?'

He walked behind for the pleasure of seeing her move, daring himself to flip the string that held the top of her two-piece. 'Is your mam in?'

'No. She's gone with me dad to Skeggy.'

He switched on the set and swung it around to get at the back. 'What's it like living in Derby?'

She leaned close, as if to learn his trade and do him out of a job. 'How do you know where we come from?'

He took his eyes from her bosom. 'I've got a file on everybody. I even know what you dream at night.'

Did she blush, or did she not? She'd been around him before. He looked at the screen. 'A snowstorm. The Rus-sians are coming.'

'I'd rather have you.'

He fiddled and synchronised till the picture became sharp. And I'd like to have you. All stations checked, he packed up his tools. 'I'm already fixed up, though.'

'Don't matter to me,' she said.

I must be mad, he thought as he walked away, unable to go with anyone while he had Eileen.

In his dreams a confusion of people were on the top-most floor of the factory. What was his mother doing there? Why was Len talking to her? They set out on a journey through the jungle. Eileen was naked, and held his hand. When he looked at his arm the skin was transparent, and he stared at the small thin red worms wriggling blindly under the surface. He told himself not to panic, there must be a cure. But he woke up with a scream that even the sea must have heard.

*　*　*

The hospital compound had so many blocks and buildings, but a passing orderly told him the ward to look into. A black nurse was emptying slops into a sink as big as a bath. 'I'm trying to find Leonard Beasley.'

'He's in there, duck, at the end. You'll see him in a wheelchair.'

He'd bought chocolates and fags at a supermarket. 'How is he?'

She had tired eyes, but her features came alive when she spoke. 'He's as well as can be expected. Is he your dad?'

'Granddad—more or less.' He liked her, so held out the chocolates. 'You 'ave these.'

'Are you sure? He can't talk, you know, but he sings.'

'Eat 'em up, sweetheart.' She put them by the sink, and he loved her because she didn't seem embarrassed. Len never ate chocolates. 'What's the doctor say, though?'

She straightened a stack of towels. 'Well, he could have another stroke any minute. He might be all right, but he'll never get over it.'

The place was full of old men, some in bed, others in wheelchairs. Maybe he should have brought whisky. Len had a blanket over his knees, and looked out of a bay window, his white hair so thin that the skin was visible

around the roots, and his face unusually clean, as if lack of worry had rinsed the skin out. When he turned, there was no light in his eyes, but he responded to his name, and took Peter's hand in a grip that he thought was crushing—if he thought anything at all.

'Are you all right, then?'

He tried to speak, and the cigarettes fell from his knees. He could use one hand, waved it in front of his face, but didn't know how to write. A half-musical noise came from his mouth.

'He's singing a little song. He's allus trying to sing "Daisy, Daisy," and things like that.'

Peter put the cigarettes on the man's bed. He wore a plaster collar, as if he had broken his neck. 'You might as well have these.'

'Thanks,' he said. 'I'm Fred Jarvis. I tell myself every morning who I am, though I don't need to yet. Anyway, I'll give old Len a puff now and again. My wife died five years ago, and they brought me here when I couldn't manage. My only regret is that we didn't have kids. I'm eighty-six, and I was in the war in France. I went over the top at Gommecourt on July first, 1916, so I've had a good innings. That nurse looks after us, though. She's a smasher!'

Peter told Len about how he managed the bungalows on the coast, but he wasn't sure he understood. He was totally cut off. The nurse brought him some tea and a cupcake, and when Peter asked her name she said it was Violet.

＊　＊　＊

'Where have you been?'

'I called on my grandfather.'

'It's six o'clock. You said you'd be back by four.'

He was fed up with this, and threw the keys on the table. 'Two hours isn't much.'

'I thought you'd had an accident.'

He tried to smile. 'Well, I didn't.'

'How was I to know?'

'Why should I?'

'Don't be bloody silly.'

'Oh, piss off. You don't own me.' He walked to the studio, like a dog going to its kennel. To pack up and go would really make him feel like a dog. In fact she was a dog for turning on him like that. Such a thought convinced him that it was time to flit—if not now, then as soon as he could. He hated himself for swearing at her. He wanted to be quiet and civilised but couldn't live up to it. All he owned would go into the suitcase, though maybe he should apologise first to prove he was civilised.

Trees with their full leaves kept light from the window, but he only needed to pull the switch down. She didn't even knock. 'Why are you in the dark?'

He took his opportunity. 'I'm sorry I swore.'

'So am I.'

She seemed to resent that he had spoken, having to be first in everything. This must be what it was like to be married. 'Come to the house for supper. I want to hear about your grandfather. You can tell me about Ingoldness later.'

She kissed him, but her mention of Len made his misery more intense. 'I'm sorry,' she said. 'I'm so stupid.'

He didn't think she had forestalled him in that, but

couldn't be sure. He was too wise to go into it. 'Of course you're not.' She always won, and he saw no reason why she shouldn't. If you were civilised, you had to let her.

'I'll get out of these baggy slacks'—he knew the meaning of her look—'and put on something nice.'

He couldn't leave, because he didn't know where he wanted to go. 'What's that music?'

Lamb chops had been grilled, potatoes baked and broccoli boiled. 'Schubert's "Unfinished Symphony." Do you like it?'

'Why isn't it finished?'

They ate at the low table, curtains drawn, a side lamp glowing on the bookcase. She put another chop on his plate. 'I'm fattening you up, you might think.'

Weight had added on, from her huge helpings and uncertain mealtimes. 'I don't mind.'

'I suppose he died. Would you like some wine?'

Not if they were going to bed.

'I recommend it,' she said.

He held the glass.

'You didn't like wine when you first came.'

She was wrong, but must have forgotten.

'I think I've corrupted you.'

He emptied the glass at one go.

'You drink it like beer.'

'I was thirsty.'

She pushed her plate aside. 'You should sip it.'

'You're supposed to drink it how you like, I reckon. It ain't whisky, is it?'

'The way you drink it, I don't think you'd know.' She looked wary, as if afraid she'd said too much, so he resisted throwing the glass in her face. To make up, she poured him some more, to find out whether or not he had learned. He slopped it into her glass. 'Let's see you sip it.'

She reached for his hand. 'Aren't we silly?'

He was hungrier than he'd thought. 'I expect so.'

'I only quarrel because I love you.'

He pondered that, while she fetched the ice cream. If that was the nearest she could get to a declaration of love, he had to be satisfied. She was almost part of him, so he was more than happy when she came back with a smile, as if looking at a man who knew he owned the world when he was with her.

After they had made love she pulled the blanket over them. 'You can stay all night.'

'I want to sleep with you every night.'

The light shone through. 'It would be nice, but I've got used to being on my own. I just like you for my boy-friend.'

There was no way to argue with somebody who knew her own mind. 'Your fancy man?'

Her breath came against him. 'That's it. My fancy man!'

'And you're my fancy woman, isn't that right, duck?'

She shivered, and came close. The tent fell in, and they struggled back to the light. 'What if your fancy woman got another fancy man?'

'First I'd kill him. Then I'd kill her. How do I know?'

'Marvellous—what with?'

'A tin opener, what else?' He kissed her, a trip around the world, from the poles to the tropics. She let herself fly, and he followed because that was where he wanted to go. Where he'd been before was nothing compared to this and yet, while making love, in a whirlpool or Milky Way, he seemed always to be himself, never unlatched from his centre, while she was not only far off from herself but as far from him as she could get. He was hardly responsible for the journeys she went on.

'You don't do yourself justice,' she said when he told her. 'I never had much life with Fred. He was ten years older, and worked too hard. Most of the time he couldn't be bothered.'

'What did you do?'

'I stewed. But I'm better now, thanks to you.'

The responsibility made him feel like a doctor.

'I've never been fucked four times in one night.'

'It'll be five, if you're not careful.'

She grasped him. 'But then, Fred was nearly fifty. Makes a difference.'

He wondered about that.

'You've come again,' she said, though he knew she hadn't.

'Potato water. I'm done for.'

She put out the light. He was aware of her walking around. The lighter went, and he got a whiff of cigarette smoke. At dawn he was pissproud and fucked her again.

By eight she was dressed for business. 'Come and get your breakfast.'

'Got any matchsticks?'

'Won't black coffee do?'

He was nearly twenty, so shaved more often. Mrs Adkin gave him a funny look, to which the only response was a wink. He knew those funny looks. We're engaged, he said, and when we're married you'll be out on your arse. But she knew better, though he didn't much care what she thought as long as his breakfast was in the bottom oven of the Aga.

'I'll be out all day. I've got to see John Scartho again. The tax man seems to be querying my expenses, though I can't imagine why, unless he thinks we put too much down for paint when you did the bungalows.'

He tackled four slices of bacon. 'Tell him to cook the books better.'

* * *

He cleared the autumn leaves, then went into town. Because it rained, he walked inside the Victoria Centre. He bought cheeses, loaves and a salami from Eileen's shopping list. The smell made him hungry, so he sat down for a cup of coffee. A few tables away he spotted his father. A trilby hat and overcoat lay on the next chair. As usual, he was well and neatly dressed.

His father winked, and came over to him. 'How goes it, then?'

He told him about his job, mentioned Len and his grandmother.

'That old bag.'

'She had a lot to put up with,' Peter reminded him.

'Who hasn't? That's what I'd like to know.'

'How are you getting on, then?'

'I'm travelling—selling electrical goods. I make more than a hundred a week. Sometimes two. Do you want lunch?'

His father reminded him of a work-shy bloke he once knew in the factory. 'No thanks.'

'Are you sleeping with this lint you work for?'

'Bollocks.'

'Just as well, I suppose.'

He had nothing else to say.

'You can come and live with us if you like.' His left eye twitched. God knows what he's got. 'Gladys works in an office. A lovely girl. She's only twenty-five. There's a spare room if you want it.'

He stood. His father was about as trustworthy as a white light warning moths off dangerous rocks. 'I don't think so.'

'You might need it one day. I must go, though, before the wardens clock my car.'

* * *

Eunice found his address and wrote to ask him for a date. Eileen brought the letter to his studio, and he set it on the table. 'Aren't you going to open it and see who it's from?'

He should have glanced through, then put it casually aside, but the postmark told him. 'I'm too busy. I'll open it later.'

'For the first time in over a year you get a letter and you're not interested who it's from. You're a bloody cool customer.'

He put on his jacket and followed her outside.

'I suppose it's from one of your girlfriends?'

'I haven't got any, you know that.' It wasn't jealousy, just that she didn't want him to have any life except with her.

'It's hard to believe.'

He thought of the misery his father had caused. 'I've got you. I don't want anybody else.'

She snapped her hand free. 'You've got me, have you?

[ 103 ]

That's what you think. Nobody has me, and you might as well know it.'

That's how it was. He didn't know whether to kill her or kiss her. While he was getting the car serviced she could steam the letter open, though he knew she wouldn't.

❊    ❊    ❊

Passing Dark Lane in Bingham, the wipers hardly cleared the glass before he had to switch them on again. If the rear window was fouled he felt uneasy at not seeing the road behind.

Beyond Grantham a vehicle carrying drainage pipes was just in front, while a black van dogged him behind. Precision and timing had become a matter of instinct, because she was fussy about the car. 'One scratch, and you're out on your neck,' but he didn't like the sort of joke that he could only make to her when they'd had a couple of drinks together.

She always used the car more at times when they were making love. Maybe it was good that he only had one thing or the other. You can't have everything, though to have both wouldn't be more than he could get used to. Perhaps it was a sign of fondness that when she didn't feel like love she at least let him have the car.

A tree showed up out of the mist like a cloud down for a breather before going on its way. Three lorries bunched in front, a 'Disabled Driver' notice in the window of one he overtook. The man in a black Vendetta hatchback must have decided that he didn't want to live, and passed the next car on a bend. He got away with it. Eileen's flash accountant dashed around in such a model, a tall and handsome smiler who never dressed in anything less than a hundred-guinea suit.

The coast was deserted, gulls over the beach and crows inland. Stalls and cafés in Skeggy were boarded up. She preferred him to say Skegness. It was a wonder the pubs weren't packed in crates and put away for winter. Grey combers came up over the sand, and people walking the promenade were wrapped against the wind.

Make number one into a paradise, she said, a snug love nest for winter. Paint this, paint that, fix that catch on the cupboard, change those curtains, make the place gleam. Stay till everything's finished. I don't care how long it takes. We'll have some lovely times when it is. I want you to be there more and more so that I can come to you. It'll be more exciting that way. I want your sperm, she said when they made it up over Eunice's letter, all you've got. She could have it. It'll keep me young, she said. She looked young already, and if she didn't on certain mornings (he wasn't daft), she more than made up for it in energy. But he wanted to walk the streets with her, go to a pub or hotel with her, go to Paris on a boat and a train. She took his hand in hers as they walked through New York.

He fell asleep early and woke at six. The kettle boiled while he fried some eggs, the rim of the yellow sun on the horizon making him feel old. Having nothing to look forward to had once been good, but now it was galling, and he knew that if Eunice came back he would get her into bed and no mistake. He had missed his chance, and in spite of knowing Eileen, felt an emptiness in his life. The horizon out at sea was like a precipice, as if should he row or swim there he would go right over.

But the day's work righted him, and when they asked in the pub if he was all right he gave the thumbs up and a smile. Didn't he have everything he wanted? Yes, but where was the rest of it? He put on his suit and went into town, the restaurant all red flock and dazzling lino, plastic lamps at the table and plaster birds on the wall. Run amok, boyo, and it was fifty p's worth of damage. An old couple sat as far away as they could get. The waitress asked what he wanted. 'Roast beef, with all the trimmings. What's your name, duck?'

The food wasn't much good, but it was nice to be served. He decided to work flat out, then go back early and visit Len. When she came to find out what pudding he wanted, he asked her name again.

'If you don't stop pestering me, I'll tell the manager.'

In a full place he'd have got no more than the smiling brush-off, but here he put the price of the meal on the table and walked out, not wanting to get into a fight.

❊    ❊    ❊

The road home was always shorter than the road out. Or perhaps it was that facing west and chasing the sun to bed took his mind off it. He hoped a miracle had happened, that Len was his touchy old self again. After laughing about times gone by, and a rant at what a bastard Len's swine of a dad had been, Peter would scour the country for his grandma to tell her what a new leaf Len had turned over. Then he'd bring her to his bedside for a good cry, and they'd stroll arm in arm to the car so that Peter could drive them home. And then what would they do, when the same old lip of the cliff was always an inch from everybody's toes?

He got mixed up. All corridors were the same. Storerooms, cubbyholes and offices branched off right and left, people too busy to be asked. He read all signs, but the ward was hiding from him, and it was such a maze that if he didn't look sharp he'd be found in a fortnight curled up and dead from starvation.

'You've cum a long way from it, mate. Let's see 'f I can tell yer where it is.'

Violet wasn't there. He walked in carrying his bag of Ingoldness rock to hand around like a spendthrift sailor, looked at by eyes from sallow faces, closed eyes behind the soft lids of near skeletons, wide-open eyes seeing only the white ceiling.

Fred Jarvis had lost his plaster collar, head lolling against the pillow. 'I spotted you in the doorway. Poor lad, I said, he's come for Len, but Len hopped it over the wire a fortnight ago.'

'Hopped it?' He'd woken up one day, dressed, and walked out whistling 'In a Persian Market,' to pick up a girl in the Wine Lodge.

He cackled. 'Got a wooden overcoat from the fifty-shilling Tailor!'

Peter felt like a balloon that somebody had stuck a pin in. 'What happened?'

'Don't look at me like that.' He righted himself. 'Shake my piller up, there's a good lad.'

He battered it on all sides. 'So he died?'

'We all will. He had another stroke. Went out singing, I will say that for him.'

He gave him a stick of rock. 'Choke on that.'

'I'd rather suck on a fag, duck.'

He left him fifteen out of his twenty. Nobody was in the office, so he wrote a note and put the rock on Violet's desk.

The metallic sun was blinding. He found his way back

to the car. A couple of dark-haired nurses, capes open and caps on, who walked by laughing and talking, would never know how much they almost made up for the bad news.

Backing out of the space, the rear left wing crunched against a concrete post.

'Hard luck, duck,' a man on crutches shouted from the sidewalk. He went into the building before Peter could tell him to fall down dead, everyone running to open doors for him.

Flakes of paint callused the concrete. He ran his fingers along corrugated tin. A real bloody mess. He stopped swearing, and sat in the car, rubbing his cold hands.

Violet came out of the doorway. 'I wanted to say thank you for the rock. My brother Lionel will love it.' She saw his glance at the damage. 'Oh, I am sorry.'

Maybe he wouldn't even go back. Elaborate plans for the big escape played on. 'Just a scrape. Do you want to come out with me tonight?'

'Me?'

The damage hypnotised him, but he assumed Eileen could claim insurance. He offered a cigarette, but she didn't smoke. 'We can go for a drink, and then have a meal.'

She laughed at how nice it would be. 'I can't tonight, though. I don't finish till half past seven. Then I've got to go home and clear up.'

'What about tomorrow?'

'That's all right.'

Working so many hours on the bungalows, with not much sleep, had worn him out, but that was no reason to scrape the car. He'd often been more tired. 'Where's convenient, then? What time?'

'Six o'clock,' she said, 'if you like. At the bottom of Birkin Avenue, where it crosses the Boulevard.'

He turned left towards town, regretting that he couldn't wind back time and fiddle his way out of the parking lot properly. The damage was done, Len was dead, but you couldn't do anything about whatever else was happening, because time still moved.

Most traffic was coming the other way. Big clouds loomed at the top of the hill, between the funnel of shop fronts as if in the sights of a rifle at a fun fair. Traffic lights beckoned him onto a roller coaster through never-ending suburbs, till he was suddenly in the middle of town and swinging along Parliament Street.

He parked the car, and walked down a covered alley towards Slab Square, a lantern shining the way through though it wasn't yet dark. But he was caught in a cakewalk, stones underfoot smoothed by millions of feet wanting to reach the lower or upper street for all kinds of reasons. Holding your breath from entrance to exit wouldn't strain the lungs very much, but a man coming towards him was not used to stepping out of the way.

The ground belonged as much to one as the other. Perhaps the grazing of the car, and hearing that Len had been carted off to the crematorium with no one to sing Jerusalem over his corpse, had raddled his senses, but when the hand came out to push him away, he knocked it upwards and grabbed the other wrist.

Recognition was immediate, though it was a long time since he had seen him in the Wine Lodge and told him to stop pressing onto the woman's foot. He lammed into him, pushed him against the wall, and put a fist under his nose so that he couldn't move without bleeding to death. His hat fell, and he caught the stink of his aftershave. 'You and your mates jumped on me outside the Royal Children, didn't you?'

'No, no. You've got the wrong 'un. It wasn't me.'

'Oh, yes it was.' He had the strength to murder him and yet, he thought, if it hadn't been for him I wouldn't have a car at the top of the yard, dented or no, nor met Eileen. 'I suppose you looked in the paper to see if I'd snuffed it. Didn't you?'

When Peter stood away, he pulled his mackintosh together and picked up his nicky hat, never lowering his gaze. Peter offered a cigarette in a voice suggesting that if he didn't take it he would really get thumped. He looked about fifty, with a thin sallow face and pale eyes, a sharp chin and a slack mouth. 'You fucking pimp. What a way to earn a living.'

He accepted the light, then fastened the white scarf back into his coat. 'It's better than working on a building site.'

A policeman came up the alley, a big Nottingham six-footer, and looked at them, as if to overhear their conversation. 'Oh, it's you. How's tricks tonight?'

'Can't grumble.'

When he'd gone Peter asked: 'A pal o' yourn?'

He spoke up clearly. 'I haven't got any in this town.'

❊   ❊   ❊

He walked into a pub wondering how many he had himself, and swilled down a pint to stop his thirst. A panorama of bottles was visible whenever he looked up from the decoration of his beer mat. The place had just opened, and a fox terrier tied to a table leg gazed at him while its gaffer brought himself down from three-o-one so cack-handedly that the darts went all over the shop. He looked happier when a bloke in an old-fashioned double-breasted suit came in and offered to play him.

Maybe the man in the alley wasn't the pimp whose mates had thrown him over a wall. That long night was out of focus, even though he drank another pint to make it come clear. If the man had appealed to the cop for help he might have ended in the nick, and mulling on this helped him into his third pint. He decided to have no more in case he got breathalysed, even though he might drive better drunk than sober.

Feeling comfortable in company that didn't acknowledge him, he ordered another, and made up his mind to stay till the towels were put on. But it was a day when his decisions were not to be trusted. Leaving half his jar un-drunk he got up and walked out, no one looking in his direction.

Rain put a shine on the street, but he didn't feel the wet as he walked to his car. The steering wheel was cold, and the radiator trembled. So did the headlamps and the bumper. To the south lay London. Cornwall was south-west. If he knew which one to drive to he would have gone. Water on the windscreen put him inside a sub-marine, waiting to see what fish would come and stare.

Rounding the island at Chapel Bar, he passed the theatres, went left at the newspaper offices, then by the Guildhall and the old Mechanics Institute. He would go to where his ladylove waited, Eileen who had jinxed him into not running away, and if there was an argument about the banged-up car it would only lead to a hot time in the bedroom afterwards.

Life was real, and would go on forever. She didn't expect him till tomorrow at the earliest. He drove through traffic, and veered off towards Mapperley, thinking that at his sudden reappearance she'd want him more than if he'd been hanging around for days.

The curving and shady road welcomed him. He should have telephoned on leaving Ingoldness so that she'd know he was on his way. She didn't like surprises, even when they were pleasant, telling him that things had to occur in their time and place, with plenty of notice beforehand. 'Makes life easier. I can fit my arrangements in properly then.'

Today he'd forgotten, but if he talked nice and tried hard, they might have the night of their lives. Before getting his wash and brush-up, he would nip in and say hello, which should be warning enough, and if there was a row, she'd calm down while he smartened up in the studio. As for the car, he'd mention that after their passionate night, and if she laid on about it, as she was bound to do, he'd give out the news that Len was dead.

This scheme, oiled along its track by the few pints, made him feel in control of his life. He whistled his way into the drive. She'd talked for months about getting a second car, and a smart little saloon gleamed by the garage. The other would be his to run around in, when it was fixed. At weekends he'd take off to any place, provided he paid for the petrol, and she might even contribute to that if an errand was involved. The idea of tackling London—two hours down the motorway—made him nervous, though he'd have a go at it sooner or later, he decided, fixing the key in the front door to go straight in.

He had never meant to be so silent and relaxed, though maybe it was the beer that let him act so that not even a cat could have gone into the house with less fuss. He might have known what he was doing but, like everything else, he knew yet didn't know, the two states so clearly divided that he moved as if in a dream.

Halfway across the hall he stopped without realising why. The gap between the two states of knowing tried to bridge itself, but he walked on, as if the pause had not happened. Even the door handle felt, momentarily, as if it burned.

He rehearsed an easy greeting, and while pushing it open, another layer of his mind informed him that his spell at the coast had produced an alteration for the better. Trust and confidence buoyed him as he went into the room, which was just as well, because the smile could turn into a laugh without much change.

❄ ❄ ❄

John Scartho had his back to the ceiling, his long, thin body like a new sort of jack from the mail order catalogue going up and down under a car that needed a wheel-changing. Either he was too busy to hear the door click, or he was at the stage where to relax would bring the invisible vehicle above crashing down on them.

The light was dazzling, but there was no need to go into the room to see the rest of it. She was always careful about drawing the curtains. In those seconds before any-one woke up, he savoured the sound effects, though it was hard to understand why—being so much in the wrong—he didn't run. Whatever he did would have been the end,

but the notion that he had been at fault in coming even this far made him feel he had nothing to lose by staying, apart from which he was so fixed by rage that it was impossible to leave.

Scartho didn't get up till Eileen brought her fist down so hard on his back that, finished or not, he rolled sideways off the sofa and onto the carpet. Peter wanted to kiss her lovely throat, fondle her neck, stroke every part of her, a loony optimism that made him hope she'd get rid of Scartho and try to talk her way clear, as if Peter was the gaffer who, having been put on short time at the factory and come home sooner than expected, had caught his wife with the lodger. He even grinned at the story, then wished he hadn't.

She straightened her skirt. 'What the hell are you doing here?'

He'd like to tell her, but no words would come. Scartho pulled up his trousers, and pushed a hand through his hair, looking startled and blank, unable to understand. 'Who the fuck *is* he?' he suddenly screamed.

She was going to laugh. It would be just like her. He wanted to laugh himself. Maybe they should all laugh. But she didn't. Nobody did. 'You've seen him before,' she said.

'Tell him to piss off,' Scartho said.

She lit a cigarette. 'Get back to your hut.'

'And how the hell did he get in? I saw you lock the door, didn't I?'

'Oh, shut up!' She turned. 'Start packing. You don't work for me any more.'

Scartho laughed. 'You do pick 'em, don't you? I suppose you just walk up and down the dole queue till you spot somebody who'll do.'

Peter felt as if he was another person looking on at himself, and only staying to see how things would end. The vicious slap across Scartho's hysterical clock went down into him with the beneficial shock of a triple whisky. But it didn't happen. She turned on him, as he might have expected: 'Are you deaf, as well as stupid?'

He had a lot to say, and his explanation was about to start, but Scartho pushed him towards the door. He jabbed back, but then turned away, becoming the single person he did not want to be.

Glasses rattled as Eileen poured a drink, and he crossed the wet grass instead of using the path. He sat in the dark. No need to put the light on, knowing where everything was. His fingers ran along the worn butt and twin barrels.

He'd frighten them. He'd have some fun. The shells were in a plastic bag under the bed. He slotted two in. If she remembered him it would be because she'd been frightened, not because she had shown him up in front of her boyfriend. Maybe he wasn't all that new. From now on you'll have to share me. One isn't enough, she'd have said. It's the done thing these days. I was meaning to tell you. Times have changed. It was the first thing he knew. He'd share no one with no one, ever.

She hadn't bothered to slot the bolt back on the door, they were so sure they'd finished him off, but even if they had barricaded themselves in he knew the house well enough for nothing to keep him out.

They stood apart, as if from kissing. 'Oh, Christ,' Scartho said, 'I thought we'd got rid of the bloody nuisance.'

They saw the gun.

'Don't think it ain't loaded.'

'It wouldn't hurt a fly,' Eileen said. 'And there's no ammunition.'

She no longer knew him, therefore she wasn't real. As he jumped off the skyscraper in New York to prove his love for her, she pulled the parachute off his back. He rolled two orange cartridges across the floor.

'Get it off him,' she said.

Scartho put his drink down. 'Not bloody likely.'

They were scared, but that was all he wanted, so now he would go, and they could do what they liked. Scartho stayed on his feet, as if waiting for the right time to tackle. He banged a football in goal every weekend.

Eileen smoked her cigarette, took a sip of her drink. They weren't frightened enough. Scartho was wary, but he wasn't frightened either. You can't frighten anybody with a gun unless you fire it. He seemed to stand for hours pointing it towards them.

'Just put the gun down,' she said.

'He's such a bright spark,' Scartho laughed, 'we'll give him a job in the office. He'll sell no end of properties with that attitude.'

'Shut up, you fool.'

He didn't thank her for it, but he no longer wanted to frighten them. He never had, but he didn't know how to go away. He'd thought to fire the gun and frighten them, but now he had to fire it before being able to leave. He no longer wanted to kill them. He had to get out, that was all.

'Peter,' she said, 'put that thing down and let's have a drink together like grown-up civilised people.'

She was onto something but, for some reason, that did it. If everything was nothing, this would be something. He raised the gun and held it firm. The safety catch was on, so there'd be no harm done. He aimed at the ceiling. It was an old farmer's gun, perhaps a hundred years old, which had been used to kill pigeons and rabbits year after year, and parts of it were almost worn through. Fred had told her, and she had told him.

The barrel exploded, and partially backfired. His scream was more horrifying than the report, as a scattering of hot steel whipped across his eyes.

✳   ✳   ✳

Going up from the river bank, where swans had honked him away from their young, he saw the roof of the small white cottage between two trees. It was miles from anywhere. The chimney smoked, so he knew she was there.

The green field was so steep that he could never reach the top. He sat in the parlour of his grandmother's house in Leicester. The familiar smells of cooking and furniture polish hemmed him in.

To live in darkness meant that you only remembered what you looked like from the days when your reflection stared at you from mirror or shop window. In those days you did not need to look, and now that you did you couldn't see. The speed of light passes you by as you feel your way around the room. Outside, light goes roaring by, but you know it is light because you recognise a voice, always too far away, that you crave to reach.

The yearning for light wouldn't leave him. If it takes a year for grief to subside, it needed the same for him to stop relying on sight to navigate his surroundings. The pain spun in futile circles like a whirlpool, only calm at the centre where there was a danger of sinking, out of which he always fought back to the edge of the whirlpool where the pain was greatest.

Life already lived was a corpse he'd bleed dry before considering the present with sufficient clarity to think of the future. His grandmother visited him in hospital after reading about the accident, and he wondered whether she wasn't making up for the way she had abandoned Len. By putting thoughts into words, the stony ground became enriched.

They sat in the solarium, and he felt warmth on his face. 'I'm doing it for lots of reasons,' she said, 'though that might be one of them.' She began to cry, at one more disaster in her life that hadn't directly touched her body. He held her hand. 'How old are you, Grandma?'

When the nurse put down more tea and went away, she said: 'I'm sixty-three. Sometimes I feel I'm ninety-nine and can't gerrin a hundred.' During the silence he sensed the racing of her mind. 'No,' she went on, 'I come to see you because you're my daughter's son, and I love you.'

'Did you love Len?'

The cup rattled on its saucer. 'I never did. I met him one night in a pub. I didn't know he was living in a men's hostel. He forced himself into my house, and it was impossible to get rid of him.'

He'd always known the world to be a hard place. The gun had gone off while cleaning, proved by the damaged ceiling. He'd held it up to look along the barrel, and his fingers got in the way. As for the bullets, he didn't know they were there. He knew nothing about guns. He'd used it as an ornament. And now look what happened, he wept to the police.

They hadn't mentioned Scartho, because Scartho had his job to think of, and he was standing for the council. Peter had come in to get some cleaning materials from the kitchen. His last feeling of admiration for Eileen was due to the speed with which, even in his agony, she had drummed the tale into him. There was nothing else she could do, which got her off with a fine. 'Ornament or not, the gun should have been licensed.' Well, it hadn't been her fault, and the magistrate must have been a friend of hers.

He told himself never to forget how good she had been to him, otherwise he wouldn't come back to life. She brought flowers and fruit.

'Shame I can't see the flowers.'

'You can smell them.' She held them close. 'And you can taste the grapes.' She put one into his mouth.

He felt tender to her, in spite of the brittle way she spoke. Maybe she sensed his concern. 'I'm sorry about all this. What a terrible thing. I can't tell you.'

He thought that if he could see her she would be an old woman. It wasn't true, but the thought went through him, so he held her hand. 'I don't need reminding.'

She left him a packet of twenty five-pound notes, and his thought of sending them back didn't last long. After all, she wasn't trying to buy him off. That's how she was. He didn't want to insult her.

When on her last visit she said she was going to marry Scartho, he laughed so loud that the nurse came to ask what was wrong.

He was still laughing when Violet visited him. He'd got one of the nurses to write. She listened while he talked, and after an hour said she must go on duty. He was mad at himself for not having let her get a word in edge-ways. She wouldn't come again, and even a letter of apology wouldn't bring her back.

His grandmother wanted to take him to Leicester by taxi, but he insisted on going by bus. It was a mistake. They shouted at each other, and people turned away when he called like a bully: 'Where's the step then, you old bag?'

He had never counted the steps between the pavement and the platform. Neither had she. Let me out! he wanted to roar, but insisted on climbing to the top deck, and cursed those passengers behind who grumbled that he ought to get a move on. Maybe they thought he was a wounded soldier from Northern Ireland. It would have made more sense.

The house was better than the one in Radford, more secure, because only the two of them were in it. She'd always had a bit of money put by. 'Thank God I never let Len know, or he would have collared the lot for drink.'

*   *   *

An island in the fog needed a light to keep all ships from its rocks, and that was bad enough, but on worse days he was an iceberg crossing the tracks of ships to sink, drifting through North Atlantic mists, sixty-foot waves washing its sides, nine tenths underwater and invincible with solid wrath and hopelessness. No warmth could thaw him on those days. He was to be avoided. He picked up his grandmother's thoughts. Best leave him be. He's only human, after all.

He was the moon and barometer all in one, wind and water pinning him into a corner he couldn't get out of, until Violet came to see him out of pity. Still, he thought, who wouldn't? His grandmother didn't like his laugh, but hoped he would get over whatever it was. And if Violet came to see him out of pity the fact seemed unimportant, because pity was priceless, and could be given away. His grandmother had pleaded for Violet to come—just to help the lad along, she said. Perhaps I know her better than Eileen.

If it was for pity's sake, he didn't care. If she came again it would be for a different reason. If she came a third time he would pity her. And if she kept on coming he would be happy. And if after a while she did it out of her own free will she might be happy as well.

There was a garden at the back, and his boots went into the hard and crusty snow. That was real. He could smell the cold, and taste the snow. Therefore, he could see it. The sound of his boots going into the snow was like walking on salt. Salt went as far as the walls, which weren't too far away. The clouds must be like mountains.

'There aren't any clouds,' Violet told him with a laugh. 'The sky's blue. There was a hard frost last night.'


Wittersham, March 30, 1986

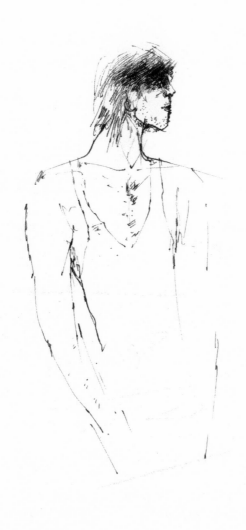